MW01490862

VOYAGES AND VOWS

A MICHIGAN MILLIONAIRES ROMANCE

KIMMY LOTH

Copyright © 2022 by Kimmy Loth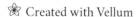

All rights reserved.

No part of this book may be reproduced in any form or by any electronic or mechanical means, including information storage and retrieval systems, without written permission from the author, except for the use of brief quotations in a book review.

❀ Created with Vellum

CHAPTER 1

Grayson tried to ignore the knot in his stomach. But it twisted and turned, not letting go. He had a quick shower, threw on joggers, and took the elevator down to the main floor of the hotel with his stomach still bothering him.

The little store was not stocked well, but it did have a small bottle of the pink stuff. He hoped it would help, but he wasn't sure anything would at this point. Maybe he should grab the bottle of vodka instead.

The woman at the counter looked at the bottle, then his face. She chuckled.

"Nervous?" she asked.

"You have no idea," he replied. Half the hotel had

been rented out for the wedding, so of course, the woman knew about it.

After she charged the overpriced bottle to his room, he escaped back upstairs and downed the whole thing.

It did not help.

He contemplated going back for the vodka but knew that wouldn't be a good idea, even if it would make him feel better.

Cinco whined from the bed, and Grayson sank down and petted the Doberman's head. He rested his snout on Grayson's thigh. He always knew when Grayson was feeling down and had been the only one Grayson confided his worries in about today.

Grayson stared out over the stormy waters of Lake Michigan. The waves were higher than normal today. It would make for stunning wedding pictures. But the clouds might also release rain that could ruin them.

That might not be a bad thing.

He immediately felt guilty for the thought. He wanted the wedding to go well, not be ruined. He owed Dani that much.

Cinco whined again, bringing his thoughts back to the inside of his hotel room instead of three hours later on the beach. "Maybe we should go for a run."

Cinco perked up, his ears alert and the stump of

his tail wagging. Grayson glanced at the clock. He'd been up way too early anyway. Sure, he'd have to shower again, but it would be worth it if the run cleared his head. Not that he expected it to help, but it would at least pass the time.

He hooked up Cinco's leash and went down the elevator. As he made his way out the back of the hotel and onto the beach, evidence of wedding set-up was everywhere.

Dani had been planning her wedding for ages, long before she even met Grayson. Her mom told him that the binder she had that held all her wedding ideas was started the year she turned eight. From then until she turned twelve, she was a bride for Halloween every year, and in high school, she simply switched to the bride of Frankenstein. Dani was unashamed of her obsession. And that was just one of the things he loved about her.

Grayson didn't need to look closely at the flowers strung around. He already knew they were white roses with pale purple lilac sprigs. He had spent hours with the florist, Dani reiterating over and over again that they had to be the perfect shade of lavender.

The chairs had been set up on the beach, white and purple ribbons hanging from them, and a tent was going up next to the chairs.

Grayson had been concerned about her being

overly obsessive when the real wedding planning finally started because he knew how much this meant to her. He had wondered if it would turn her into a different person.

But he never once saw her lose her temper with anyone. She'd shed a few tears when she found her budget wouldn't cover the cake she wanted—a seven-tiered monstrosity from a baker she'd been following on Instagram for years. But she found a less expensive local baker and toned down the cake.

Grayson went behind her back, canceled the order, and paid for the Instagram baker. He couldn't wait to see her face when she saw it.

There had been a few other things like that, but Grayson took care of them all. He wasn't about to let her dream wedding become anything less than she'd imagined. There was nothing he wouldn't do for her. She was his best friend and had been since their freshman year in college. She deserved the world, and he did everything he could to make sure she got it.

He wasn't sure when he'd fallen in love with her. It might've been that first night they met when he saw her across the room at one of the frat parties. It might've been the nights he spent tutoring her in biology. Though he suspected it was the night he kissed her for the first time.

He'd never forgotten that night. They'd been a

little tipsy from a party and were out walking the campus. It was still early fall and not quite cold. She'd been telling him all about her dream wedding, and he couldn't help himself. He kissed her.

Which was stupid really. What young college frat boy kisses a girl who just told him about the wedding she'd been planning since she was eight?

He had.

And here he was.

At the wedding that was exactly the same as she'd always wanted.

Down to the heavily perfumed lilac sprigs.

He bounded down the sand with Cinco, eyeing the clouds. This would not bode well for the wedding. After they got farther away from the hotel, Grayson let Cinco off his leash, and he went racing out into Lake Michigan. Grayson hadn't foreseen that. Though he should've.

He was too distracted by the pain in his stomach and the wedding.

It would take forever to clean Cinco up. He didn't have time for that. As it was, he barely had time to get back and get ready.

He wished the day would stretch on forever and never get to the wedding. Then things would continue on just like they always had.

Instead, Dani was getting married.

And he wasn't the groom.

CHAPTER 2

So far, Dani's wedding day was nothing like she'd imagined. She'd woken up late to a massive headache and an overcast sky that threatened to rain buckets on her beautiful day. She took a couple of Tylenol and a hot shower. She would not let something like a few clouds ruin the day she'd been imagining. She had a backup plan and a backup plan to her backup plan.

Dani had been planning her wedding since she was eight. By the time she turned fifteen, she knew she wanted it on June twelfth (a day that typically had seventy-five-degree weather and historically no rain) on the beach in Glen Arbor. All of the details were carefully crafted. It should've been fairly easy to execute—the planning stages had gone well, thanks to

Grayson—but today nothing was going right, and she couldn't figure out why.

She sat in her beautiful dress that somehow didn't look quite right. It was a sleek dress, long and flowing, and her long blond hair was up in a French twist.

Surrounded by three of her close friends, she worried this day wouldn't live up to her expectations. Now that it was here, she felt let down. It was the clouds. It had to be the clouds. If it rained, the day would be ruined.

A knock sounded on the door.

"Is she decent?" Grayson asked, and the tightness in her chest relaxed a hair. He could fix this. Well, maybe not the clouds, but at least he'd be able to make her feel better.

"She looks like she's about to ball buckets," Stacy said. "But she's fully clothed, if that's what you're asking."

Grayson popped in, and Dani turned around, meeting the eyes of her best friend. She supposed she wasn't very good company at the moment. She'd tried hard to not be a bridezilla since she got engaged, but today she definitely was.

As the bridesmaids left, Stacy paused and placed a hand on Grayson's chest, whispering something in his ear. Dani didn't know what it was, but she didn't like the way Stacy touched him. Not that Dani had any say over who touched Grayson. Especially after today, but the green-eyed monster always reared its ugly head where Grayson was concerned.

Grayson looked dashing in his man of honor suit. He'd been there with her through it all, and she didn't know what she would do without him. He'd been like her big brother all through college and beyond. He was incredibly good-looking, and on more than one occasion, her mom asked why she was with Jeremy instead of Grayson, but she loved Jeremy.

Besides, she was nowhere near Grayson's league, and she never would be. So she never let herself have feelings for him. That would only lead to heartbreak. She had made a lot of sacrifices for Jeremy, but they were worth it. She wanted kids, and he didn't, and she'd resolved herself to that. It was okay because she loved him.

Jeremy had been a little uncomfortable with Grayson as her man of honor, but he'd gotten used to it. He didn't like all the wedding planning stuff, and Grayson went with her so Jeremy didn't have to. They didn't even bother correcting the vendors when they assumed Grayson was the groom.

Dani stared at the clouds. Her day was about to be ruined.

"It's going to rain," Dani whined, trying to keep the tears in. Why did there have to be clouds today? It was the one thing that was completely out of her control, but she had researched the weather and found a day that historically never had rain.

Grayson chuckled. "It might. But if it rains, you have a tent with sidewalls, and no one will get wet."

This was true. She'd made sure they were prepared for everything. But still. This was not how she wanted her wedding to go. She didn't want to be in the tent.

Dani tried not to stick her lip out and pout. "I want my wedding on the beach with full sun."

"And have people drenched in sweat?" Grayson asked.

"I am wearing prescription-strength deodorant. I really don't care." She heard the cattiness in her voice, but Grayson didn't comment.

He crouched in front of her. "Listen, Jamie said overcast is better for pictures anyway. And he's had some photo shoots where it started pouring in the middle of everything, and they've been his best ones."

She noticed his careful use of language. "I doubt those were weddings."

Grayson leveled her with a look. He was good at calling her out on her crap. "Stop pouting. This is your wedding day, and it'll be perfect. Even if it rains. As long as you don't freak out. Come on, let's go make your dreams come true."

He held out a hand, and she grasped his. Grayson always knew the right thing to say. She took a deep breath. This was a day she'd remember forever, and she wanted to have good memories of it, not ones where she stressed the whole time. He was right. As usual.

Dani tucked her arm into Grayson's. He kissed her on the cheek, and a slight thrill ran up her spine. She ignored it. Today she would become Jeremy's wife, and she would have to stop mooning over a man she could never have.

Not only was Grayson her man of honor, but he was also walking her down the aisle. Dani's father died several years ago. A fact for which she'd been grateful. He had been a cruel and abusive man.

"Are you sure you're ready for this?" he asked.

Dani beamed up at him. "I've been ready for this for years."

And she had.

But she still couldn't help the feeling of dread in her stomach.

CHAPTER 3

They walked out onto the beach, and everything was exactly as Dani had envisioned. The lilacs and roses were perfect, and the chairs were all situated just right. Exactly fifty-two guests. Everybody looked incredible as they stood and waited for her to walk down the aisle. Even the clouds had parted and let the sun out. No rain on the horizon.

She had been worried for nothing.

Her dreams were coming true.

She met Jeremy's eyes. Her smile widened. There he was, her perfect groom. He didn't want a big wedding, but he'd been so patient with her. Love swelled in her breast as she stared at him.

No smile crossed his lips. In fact, he looked a little

ill. Her own smile faded, and she swallowed.

That wasn't at all how she'd imagined her groom's face would look when he saw her in her dress for the first time. Tears, a wide smile, unabashed love, but not ill. Dani gripped harder to Grayson's arm, but he didn't seem to notice anything.

She glanced up at Jeremy again, but there was still no smile. He had not wanted to get married. In fact, he'd been clear when they started dating that he'd never get married, but he'd come around. He knew how important this was to her, and she loved him for it. Perhaps that's all this was. Nerves about marriage. He'd get over it.

She walked slowly down the aisle. Grayson kissed her cheek and leaned over and whispered in her ear. "See, no rain. I'm a miracle worker."

He handed her off to Jeremy, who wouldn't look her in the eye.

"Are you okay?" she whispered. She needed him to be. This was their wedding day. They should both be thrilled.

He shook his head, and Dani's throat clogged up.

She took a deep breath and let it out again. This would be okay. All they had to do was make it through the ceremony, and she could get a glass of champagne in his hands. He'd relax, and everything would go as planned. She doubted anyone but her noticed Jeremy's nervousness, and if they did, well, the groom was supposed to be nervous, right?

The pastor she'd known her whole life quickly went through his spiel. Dani barely even heard it. Next to her, Jeremy was shaking so badly, she was sure everyone could see. She couldn't believe he was this nervous. She thought back to the past few days. He hadn't been acting weird at all. Though she'd barely seen him. She and Grayson had been making sure everything was ready for the wedding.

Her pastor smiled down at her. "Do you take this man to be your lawfully wedded husband, to love him and cherish him for as long as you both shall live?"

"I do," Dani said without hesitation. She couldn't believe she was about to be married. A wife.

"And do you take this woman to be your lawfully wedded wife, to love her and cherish her for as long as you both shall live?"

Jeremy didn't say anything for a long moment. Then that long moment became uncomfortable. She tried to meet his eyes, but he was staring at their intertwined hands.

"Jeremy," she hissed. "It's your turn."

He finally looked at her with pain behind his baby blues. "I'm sorry. I can't do this."

He turned and walked away, down that perfect sandy aisle and back into the hotel beyond. Tears clogged her throat once again, but she didn't let them out. There was dead silence on the beach, except for the waves, and the sound roared in her ears.

She didn't know what to do, where to go, or who to look at. Dani wasn't a public crier, so tears didn't run. But how she wanted to scream, yell, and hit something. Her perfect day had just been ruined. Yes, she was going to miss Jeremy. She loved him, but right now she could only muster the energy to be upset by the wedding. If she thought too hard about the future, she'd completely lose it.

Grayson was at her side in seconds, and he whispered in her ear.

"Dani bear, I know this is your special day, and I don't want to see it ruined. Will you let me help you?"

"What do you mean?" she whispered back, the tightness in her throat lessening. Grayson would help her. He always did. She was so grateful he was here, but she didn't see what he could possibly do to fix this. Unless he was about to run after Jeremy and make him come back and marry her.

"Just say yes, and we'll figure out the details later." She had no idea how he could be so calm.

"I don't understand."

He should be long gone, racing after the man she was supposed to marry. Grayson was persuasive.

Jeremy would listen to him. He had to. Dani had been waiting too long for today for it to end like this.

"I know, but people are watching, and if we don't do this quickly, things will get awkward."

"Things are already awkward." She couldn't believe she'd just been left at the altar. She really was going to puke. That would make this even better. Instead of beautiful pictures, there would be ones of her alone, with puke all over her dress. How had things gone so wrong, so quickly?

Grayson squeezed her hand again. "Seriously. Just say yes, and your day will still be salvageable."

"Okay, yes, go get him." She nudged Grayson in the arm and looked to the path Jeremy had taken moments ago.

Instead of running off, Grayson dropped down on one knee.

CHAPTER 4

Grayson had no idea what he was doing. He just knew he couldn't let that douchebag ruin Dani's wedding. She had shared with him Jeremy's hesitation to get married, but Grayson didn't think the guy would leave her at the altar.

He didn't know if Dani would play along or not. If she ran from him, he wouldn't care. He just wanted to give her the opportunity to have her perfect day. She deserved it. After she'd been there for when his sister died and all those nights he called her, whining about how hard some of his classes were. She was his rock and he wasn't about to let her down now.

He looked up into her horrified eyes and spoke from the heart. He didn't know any other way to do this. He spoke loudly so that everyone else would hear. They had to make this believable. Which wouldn't be all that hard, considering how he felt about her.

"Dani, you and I have been best friends a long time. And I've loved you for nearly all of those years. You're my best friend and the one that I want to come home to every night. I know this is unusual, but I've kept my mouth shut because I didn't want to interfere in your relationship with Jeremy. I can't hold back any longer. I love you, and I want you to be my wife. Will you marry me?"

A few gasps came from the crowd, and one of the bridesmaids squeed. But Grayson didn't pay any attention to them. He had eyes only for Dani.

He spoke from the heart, but she didn't know that. She probably assumed he was just acting. But it didn't matter. What mattered was that her wedding wasn't ruined. And maybe he wasn't exactly what she wanted —she'd made that clear on numerous occasions, but at least, she'd have her dream wedding.

But only if she said yes.

She stared at him for a long moment, and he could see the questions behind her eyes. This wouldn't work if she tried to make sense of things.

Finally, she nodded. "Yes. I will marry you."

He whooped, stood, and wrapped his arms around her, spinning her in a circle. He whispered in her ear. "We don't have to sign the marriage certificate. But this way, your big day is still exactly what you want. Well, minus the groom." He caught a glimpse of the crowd. Dani's mom had tears running down her cheeks, and a few of Jeremy's friends were leaving.

"You make a better groom anyway," she whispered back, and his heart swelled. "Thank you."

He liked the feeling that he could give her things no one else could. He set her down and turned to face the pastor. This was the man who baptized Dani as a baby. Grayson just hoped he'd go for this.

"Dani, this is highly unusual," he said, his face concerned.

She gripped Grayson's hand. "I know, but Grayson is my best friend. I feel the same way he does about me. I just never admitted it. You've seen us. Everyone always assumes we're a couple. We were just too afraid to admit it to each other for fear of ruining our friendship."

"If that's really what you want."

The pastor looked like he wanted to argue but didn't, and Grayson let out a breath of relief.

Dani nodded eagerly.

The pastor didn't go through all of his speech again. He just skipped straight to the "I dos."

"Do you take this man to be your lawfully wedded

husband, to love him and cherish him for as long as you both shall live?"

Dani squeaked out an "I do."

Grayson tried not to read too much into it. She didn't feel the same way about him, but he'd always wanted more. He'd hinted at it a couple of times, but she'd never responded.

"And do you take this woman to be your lawfully wedded wife, to love her and cherish her for as long as you both shall live?"

"I do." Grayson spoke the words loudly so everyone could hear. He wanted people to know that Dani was desired and loved, not jilted.

"Now you may kiss the bride." The pastor winked at Grayson.

He turned to Dani and stared into her beautiful green eyes. He took her face in his and hesitated. He didn't want to do anything she didn't want. But if he didn't kiss her, this wouldn't look right, and her wedding would be ruined anyway. Everyone would know that she wasn't really married, and it was all fake.

Kissing her again was something he'd always wanted to do, but he'd never envisioned it to be on her wedding day in front of several dozen people, most of whom didn't even know him.

He brought his lips to hers. He needed to make

this long enough to make it authentic but not too long as to make things awkward with her. He was thinking about this far too much.

Her lips were soft under his, and he was surprised to find her kissing him back. He moved his mouth softly against hers, and she wound her arms around his neck, pulling him closer.

He obliged and held her tight against him. Her lips parted, and he pulled away, not wanting to take this past a point of no return. He loved her, but he wasn't about to lose his best friend in the process.

She looked a little shocked.

"Smile," he muttered and released her, but grabbed her hand instead.

Grayson smiled out at the crowd, and Jamie let out a whoop before bringing his camera to his face.

Grayson led her back down the aisle, and friends and family congratulated them along the way. A few seemed bewildered, but Grayson didn't care.

Blake smacked him on the back as he passed. "You waited long enough, didn't you?"

Grayson didn't respond.

Dani had a forced smile plastered on her face. He could tell, even if no one else could.

He was happy about this, but she clearly wasn't.

CHAPTER 5

*D*ani shouldn't have enjoyed that kiss.

Her fiancé just left her at the altar. The man she was planning on spending the rest of her life with. The man she loved. And he'd just betrayed her in the worst way. Even though Grayson had rescued her, she still felt like crawling out of her skin.

She brought her fingers to her lips. That kiss.

That had been Grayson kissing her.

Grayson! The man who'd been the big brother she'd never had. The man who had been with her every step of the way as she navigated adulthood. He was her best friend, and his kiss made her toes curl. This was wrong, and she didn't know how she felt about it.

He'd kissed her once before, back in college. But

they'd had too much to drink, and neither one talked about it the next day. It was a sloppy drunk kiss. This kiss was toe-curling and one she'd never forget. Perhaps she was just reading too much into it because she'd dreamed of this day for years but had never let it happen.

Because as much as she loved Grayson, she would never be good enough for him. She was lucky he was her best friend. That was something she could never lose. But this...

This was the stuff of break-up legends.

If she allowed him to kiss her like that again, he'd break her heart.

Grayson held tightly to her hand and led her to the bride's room.

"What are we doing here?" she asked. They should be heading to the reception.

"I thought you might need a moment before we are ambushed by your family and friends."

Her mind was swirling with everything that had happened, and nothing was making sense yet. She stared down at her perfectly manicured fingernails. They were pale pink with French tips. But she shouldn't be thinking about her nails right now. She just married her best friend. What happens now?

Grayson hesitated for a moment, taking a breath. "We need to get our stories straight."

She jerked her head up.

"Stories?" She didn't want to think about their stories. What she wanted to do was rip her dress off, drink a bottle of champagne, and cry the rest of the night. But she still had the reception to get through.

Grayson placed his hands on her shoulders and stared deep into her eyes. For a second, she thought he was going to kiss her again, and part of her wanted him to. When he kissed her, all thoughts disappeared. It was just her and him, and nothing else mattered.

But that was stupid. He might sleep with her tonight but then be gone the next morning. Grayson never had long-term girlfriends, and she was about to become another broken heart.

"Our stories. People will want to know how this happened, and I have an idea."

"Good, cause I've got nothing." She could hear the tremor in her own voice.

He chuckled. "Relax. I've got this. Trust me."

"I always do."

"We should say that we've both been in love with each other for years but had no idea the other one felt the same way, and neither of us said anything out of respect for your relationship with Jeremy. We have no idea where things will lead from here, but we plan on figuring that out during the honeymoon."

"Honeymoon," Dani said. The cruise she'd planned down to the minute. She had every excursion picked out and where they would stand each night and watch the sunset. It was supposed to be a week of wedded bliss, and now it was ruined. "We're not going on a honeymoon."

Grayson creased his eyebrows. "Why not? It's the perfect place for you to recover from this. I'll book my own room, and we'll spend the evenings getting drunk and talking trash about Jeremy. Besides, it's all paid for already."

She wanted to laugh at his statement, but it was too raw. She was going on her honeymoon without her husband. She scrimped and saved every penny she had. This honeymoon was the biggest splurge she'd ever made, and even then, she booked a cheap interior room and only three shore excursions.

And Grayson was just going to book a room like it was nothing. He'd probably get a suite.

But she didn't want to go alone, and he was right. It would be the perfect place to relax and recover from Jeremy's betrayal. Plus, it would keep her away from annoying family and friends who would want to rehash things.

"Okay. I like that story." She fluffed her dress out. "Can I hang out in your room sometimes? I assume you'll have a huge balcony."

"You're welcome anytime. Are you ready?" he asked.

She shook her head. "But I have to be." She blinked away a few tears. Her life with Jeremy was over. She was going to miss his family. His mom had become a second mother to her. She wondered what she was thinking now.

Grayson moved past her and picked up her lipstick. He smudged a little on the edge of his lip. It wasn't totally obvious, but someone would notice.

"What are you doing?" she asked.

"Making it look like we just spent the last fifteen minutes making out."

She rolled her eyes and grabbed his hand, glad things were still normal between them. "Come on, Casanova, we've got a crowd to deceive."

They'd made their way down the halls of the hotel, hand in hand. They'd held hands many times before, but it was always out of necessity to keep from getting lost or something. This felt different. They were *married*, though not officially. Still, they had to make it look like it.

She wasn't sure how she'd keep it together during the reception, but it wouldn't be the first time she had to keep her emotions hidden.

They walked into the reception tent, and she stopped. The cake was seven tears, a perfect ivory with edible flowers that looked so real she could barely tell they weren't.

"That's not the cake I ordered," she said.

Grayson gave her one of his devastating smiles. The one that made all the girls at college swoon. Including her.

"I know. But it is the one you designed." His voice was soft and low.

"How?" she asked. It was the cake of her dreams and way, way too expensive.

"I canceled the one you didn't want and ordered this one."

"But it wasn't in the budget." Her voice caught in her throat.

Grayson squeezed her hand. "But it was the one you wanted."

Something threatened to erupt in her chest, but before she could process it, her mother descended on her.

"Oh, sweetie, I'm so happy for you." She flung her arms around Dani, and Dani forgot all about the cake.

CHAPTER 6

*G*rayson leaned against one of the tent poles and watched Dani laughing with her girl-friends. He'd worried that she wouldn't even be able to smile at the reception, but she'd taken right to it. They'd told their silly made-up story several times already, and everyone bought it.

Dani's mom was thrilled.

Grayson knew she'd never really liked Jeremy, but he hadn't realized how much until now. She kept coming around to him, squeezing his hand and wiping tears from her eyes.

Jamie clapped Grayson on the shoulder, his camera held tight in his other hand. "I don't believe that BS story for a second. What's the real deal?"

Grayson ran a hand over his face. Of course Jamie

would notice. He was close to Grayson, and on more than one occasion, he asked why Grayson was letting Dani marry Jeremy. He hadn't spent a whole lot of time with Dani, but Dani wanted him to be her wedding photographer. It wasn't something Jamie did often, but he did it because she was a friend. "Do you think everyone else believes it?"

"I do. But you forget that I did the fake marriage thing with Bethany." Jamie's situation was different. He needed Bethany to get custody of his son, and they fell in love.

"That's right, you did. Look at how that turned out."

"You hoping for something similar?" He raised his camera and got a shot of Blake and Paige dancing.

Grayson swallowed. He'd never really admitted this to anyone. "The story might be made up for Dani, but it's very real for me. I've been in love with her since college."

Jamie whistled. "I knew it. And you were willing to let her marry another guy? That takes guts, man. I'm impressed."

"I just want her to be happy."

"Are you going on the honeymoon with her?"

"Yeah." He wondered what that would mean for the both of them. Things could change. Maybe for the better. Hopefully for the better.

Jamie aimed his camera for a few shots of Dani dancing with the flower girl. It was Jeremy's niece, but they'd still stayed. Not a single member of his family said a word to Grayson though.

"Well, then you've got a week to convince her to stay married to you. I wish you luck."

"Thanks." He hadn't had much time to think about it, but Jamie was right. Grayson wanted to be married to Dani, and this could be the perfect opportunity to bring up that their friendship could be so much more if they let it.

The wedding planner approached Dani and whispered something in her ear. Dani made her way over to Grayson. "It's time for the bouquet and garter toss."

Grayson gripped her hand. "We can skip the garter toss. I doubt people will even notice."

He didn't want to make her uncomfortable, and as much as he wanted to slide his hand up her calves and thighs, this was not the time to be doing that. He needed to show her that he respected her and her boundaries.

She let out a breath. "Okay. Thanks. I'm so ready to go. I don't know if I can keep myself together much longer."

"Okay. I'll work on getting you out of here."

He let Dani go up on the stage by herself, and

women gathered around. Dani laughed and teased the crowd. Then she spun around and tossed the bouquet. A pretty young woman caught it, and everyone cheered.

He rushed up to the stage. "Let's get out of here before anyone asks us to do something you don't want." There were quite a few wedding traditions that people could invoke—the garter only being one.

She nodded. "Okay."

Within minutes they were running out the door, surrounded by sparklers and flying bird seed. Before he knew it, they were at the door to her suite. He had to stay there tonight, or people would get suspicious, but it wouldn't be the first time they spent the night together. They fell asleep plenty of times watching movies or lying in a hammock on a summer's afternoon. It'd never once been romantic.

Tonight would be no different. He planned on holding her while she cried. Dani was a pro at keeping her emotions in check, and he knew she had to be dying inside. It was only a matter of time before she lost it. Before she could push the door open, he swept her into his arms.

She squeaked. "What are you doing?"

"What does it look like I'm doing?"

She laid her head on his shoulder. "We're not really married."

"Still, it's my job as the man of honor to make sure you get the wedding you always dreamed of."

He pushed the door open and carried her inside. She patted him on the chest. "You did do that. Thank you. Minus Jeremy, it was perfect."

"Well, considering what Jeremy did, I'd say I'm a better groom than him anyway." He wondered how the next week would go. If he'd manage to convince her to sign that marriage certificate or not. He wasn't even sure he wanted her to. Well, he definitely wanted her to, but if they were going to make it as a couple, he wanted it to happen naturally, not be forced.

He set her gently onto the bed, and her face deflated.

"It's over," she said. "And I have no idea what the rest of my life will be like. I'd always imagined Jeremy in it."

Then she burst into tears.

His job as man of honor still wasn't over.

CHAPTER 7

*D*ani stared out the window of the plane. They were flying first class. Grayson had switched her seats without telling her. When she argued, he told her there was no way he was flying in coach, and he wanted to sit next to her.

"You sure you don't want the window?" she asked. Secretly, she hoped he said no, but also, he was paying for this. He deserved to have the window.

"Positive. You've never had that view. I have."

She blinked at him. As close as they were, she'd never really taken part in his world. Every time they hung out, they'd kept things low-key. She'd gone up to Mackinac with him and his friends a few times, but this—flying first class—was something she'd never done before. She'd only flown on a plane a couple of times and always ended up in a middle seat.

She grew up in a home with an alcoholic, abusive father and an uneducated mother. After her dad lost his job because of his alcoholism, her mom worked two jobs just to pay rent. Dani started babysitting at age twelve and got her first job at McDonald's at fourteen. By the time she reached her junior year in high school, she'd been working thirty hours a week and busted her butt to get college scholarships. She'd scored a full ride to Michigan, and between her scholarship money, a work-study job, and loans, she'd made it through two years of college before she had to drop out and take care of her mom because her dad died and her mom fell apart. In spite of the issues, she and her dad had, her mom loved him and couldn't get out of bed for weeks and hadn't been the same since.

Dani managed to land a job as a vet tech—not her dream of being an actual veterinarian, but they'd managed to scrape by. She'd been paying several of her mom's bills, but that was only because Jeremy paid all of theirs. She wouldn't be able to afford to help her now. Also, she didn't know what she was going to do now. She worked for Jeremy. He was an actual veterinarian. He left her at the altar; would he fire her as well?

Oh, what was she thinking? Even if he didn't fire her, she couldn't keep working for him.

She swallowed, and dread settled in her stomach.

That was a problem she could think about after the honeymoon was over.

Grayson knew some of her money issues, but she'd done a pretty good job at hiding it from everyone else. Even Jeremy didn't know the whole of it because she was excellent at managing her money and had started a wedding savings account the second she started babysitting.

But it still wasn't enough for her to get everything she dreamed of.

Yet. It had all been exactly how she'd imagined. Grayson had done more than just book her favorite cake designer.

He squeezed her hand, and she looked over at him. "Are you okay?" he asked.

She shook her head. She didn't know if she'd ever be okay again. "What am I going to do? Jeremy and I share an apartment and a car. I don't want to be alone again."

"You don't have to be alone. I'll be here for you as long as you want. You can even move into my place."

He was being ridiculous. "You live three hours from me."

"I'll get an apartment in town." He shrugged.

"You don't have to do that." He was always so good at taking care of her. For him to offer to move here was too much.

"Dani, as far as everyone is concerned, we're married. If you want to keep appearances up, we can do that. I'm not dating anyone. You're my best friend. I'd do anything for you."

She let out a sigh. It wasn't a bad idea, but she didn't want to drag this out. "Maybe I should just move in with my mom. She needs the help anyway." Dani actually didn't see how they'd be able to afford anything else.

Grayson frowned but didn't reply.

"I do appreciate everything you are trying to do. It's not your fault my life fell apart."

He nodded. "I know. But for the next week, it's my job to make sure you don't cry."

"What if I need to cry?"

"Then I will hold you and wait no more than thirty minutes. After that, I reserve the right to do whatever it takes to make you stop."

She snorted. "Okay. Thanks, Grayson. I really do want to enjoy this trip."

"You haven't taken a big vacation for as long as I've known you. You deserve this."

He was right. She would do her best during the trip to forget all about Jeremy, even if that meant going heavy on the alcohol. She'd never been much of a drinker because of her father and also because it was expensive.

But she figured one trip wouldn't hurt. She would indulge during the cruise because, after that, she had to face a new reality.

"Okay. You better bring your A-game because I expect this to be the best week of my life."

He chuckled. "That sounds more like it." He waved over a flight attendant. "My wife and I are on our honeymoon. Can we get two glasses of champagne, please?"

The woman smiled. "Of course. Congratulations."

Grayson waited until the woman was out of earshot. "Let's milk this for all it's worth, shall we?"

Dani nodded. She just hoped she wouldn't regret this.

Because for the next week, at least, she'd be Grayson's wife.

After that, she'd be single for the first time in eight years.

CHAPTER 8

*G*rayson watched Dani carefully as they exited the plane. She was acting like everything was okay, even though he knew it wasn't. He wanted her to remember this cruise with fondness, not pain. And if Grayson played his cards right, he might turn the worst thing that ever happened to her into the best thing. He wasn't sure how to do that yet, but he'd figure it out.

As soon as the plane landed, Grayson called for a driver. By the time they grabbed their bags, they found the man with a sign for McBride by the door. Grayson waved to him and reached for his bag.

"Take my wife's, please," Grayson said.

Dani jerked her head around. "We don't have to keep it up, you know."

He sighed but didn't correct himself. The driver extracted Dani's bag from her, and they followed him out to a waiting limo. Technically, she was his wife, and he didn't want her to forget it. He wanted to use this time to spoil her and show her what life with him would be like.

Dani motioned to the car as the driver threw her bag into the trunk. "Why did you get a limo?"

Grayson wasn't sure what would bother her more: him telling her that he always got a limo or telling her that it was because of their honeymoon. He decided to stick with the current theme.

"It's your honeymoon. Everyone uses a limo on their honeymoon."

She swallowed but didn't argue with him. His money had always bothered her, and he wasn't sure why.

He waited for her to get into the car and then slid in behind her. He sat close and flung his arm across the seat behind her. She stayed tense the entire ride to the port.

Grayson tried to keep up the conversation, but she wasn't having it.

The driver dropped them off at the entrance. Grayson tipped him generously and asked that he make sure the bag porter got a twenty.

The driver nodded vigorously.

"What's happening to our bags?" Dani asked as he grabbed her hand and led her away from the car.

"He'll get them to where they need to go." Grayson led her into the crowded room and headed toward the short line, but Dani stopped him.

"Where are you going?" she asked.

"I got a suite," he said, pointing to the sign over the shorter line, which was for suite guests.

"But I didn't." Her face was a mask of pain. He didn't want this to be more difficult for her. "It doesn't matter. I'll make sure they let you check in with me."

"Grayson," Dani warned. He couldn't figure out why she was fighting him on this.

"What?" He pulled her aside and met her worried eyes.

She dropped her gaze and chewed on her bottom lip. "I don't want to pretend like I'm you."

"Why not? This trip is all make-believe anyway. Right? Embrace it, and let me take care of you."

"Not by throwing your money around."

He sighed and thought about how to handle this. He hated waiting in lines. In fact, most of the time he paid extra to make sure he never stood in a line. But this was Dani.

"Fine," he said and moved back to the long line with her.

"What are you doing?" she asked.

"Waiting in the long line with you." He wasn't leaving her side this whole trip. He wanted her to know that he'd always be there for her.

"But you don't have to." She wouldn't meet his eye, and he stared at her lips. He wondered what she would do if he kissed her again. He hadn't stopped thinking about their wedding kiss.

"I'm not leaving you alone," he said. "By the time we get through this line and into your room, it'll be a few hours. This is your first cruise, and I'm going to be with you through it all."

Her face softened. "Thank you."

Thirty minutes later, the line hadn't moved more than a few feet. Dani shifted back and forth on her feet and nudged him. "Maybe I need to eat crow."

"What do you mean?" he asked.

"I mean, maybe I don't want to wait in this line for two hours." Her voice had gone sugary sweet. It was the voice she used when she wanted something from him and not one he heard often.

He studied her for a second. "Okay. But under one condition." He wasn't going to let her get away with fighting him on everything he tried to do for her this trip.

"What's that?"

He stared deep into her eyes and grabbed both of

her hands. He wanted her to know he meant business. "I'm still doing my duty as man of honor, and that's to make sure you have an amazing time on this trip. I have money, and I'm going to spend it, and you aren't going to argue with me about it again. I'll buy you drinks, take you on expensive shore excursions, and make sure I get you a necklace or ring at the jewelry shops in port. You'll pick out things you like and not ask about the price. If we move to the short line, that's you giving me your promise that you'll let me spoil you without argument."

She chewed on her lip and stared at the long line in front of them.

He brought his hand up to her chin and forced her to look at him. There was a mixture of pain and desire in her eyes that he didn't fully understand.

"And one more thing."

She snorted. "Just one?"

He smiled. "Just one. For the duration of this trip, when we are in public, you are my wife, not my friend."

"But we'll have separate rooms."

At this point, he knew he won. "We'll tell people I snore."

She chuckled, took one more look at the long line, and ducked under the rope. She was ten steps away before he registered what happened.

42

From now on, he wasn't holding anything back.

CHAPTER 9

*D*ani bounced from one foot to the next as she waited for Grayson to check in. He seemed entirely at ease with the whole process.

Dani felt irritated and she couldn't figure out why. Maybe that was because he got his way with the line. She should have let him spoil her, but for some reason, it made her incredibly uncomfortable.

"You managed to snag one of the last rooms on board," the lady said with a simpering smile at Grayson.

"I know. I wanted a bigger suite, but that was all they had left." He winked at her.

Why did he have to turn on his charm like that with her? Grayson would end up with her phone number if he wasn't careful.

"Well, I hope you enjoy your cruise anyway." She was entirely too perky about the whole situation. And pretty. Ugh. Where had this jealousy come from? Though, if she were honest with herself, it wasn't new. She was always jealous of the women who grabbed Grayson's attention.

"I'm sure I will."

The woman handed him his room key and a lanyard. "Lunch for elite members is on the third deck, front dining room. We set sail at four p.m. sharp, and I recommend the eighteenth-floor port side for a nice view. Though your balcony will have a lovely view as well."

Dani took note of the eighteenth-floor idea as she would have no such view.

Grayson reached behind her and placed a hand on her back. "I know this is highly unorthodox, but my best friend is also on this cruise and would like to check in with me."

Best Friend. Just before this Grayson had told her that he would be referring to her as his wife. And now she was his best friend. Maybe he wanted that number after all. She shouldn't be jealous. Grayson would totally forget about this random woman in Miami. She had no right to be jealous.

But of course she was.

The woman looked down her nose at Dani.

"You're right. That is unorthodox. She will need to get in the other line."

Grayson slid a fifty her direction. "Please."

The woman glanced around, pocketed the fifty, and grinned. "I'll see what I can do."

Dani nearly argued with him about the bribe but then remembered the deal they made. Though that deal didn't include calling her his best friend.

Dani handed over her ID, and the woman hurried through her check-in. She handed Dani the room key with no lanyard and said nothing about lunch.

"Did you get her number?" Dani asked as they left the desk. She hadn't seen anything like that, but maybe the woman had been sneaky about it.

"What are you talking about?" He looked like he had no earthly idea what would give Dani that idea.

Dani gave a forced grinned and nudged him. "Oh, come on, you were totally picking her up."

Grayson looked down at her, his face a mask of horror. "What are you talking about? I was not."

"I thought I was your wife. And suddenly, in front of a pretty girl, I'm your best friend." Dani knew her voice came out whiny, but she couldn't help herself.

His cheeks reddened, and he rubbed the back of his neck. "Oh yeah. It would be weird when we're checking in to have two different rooms. But from now on…" He let his words trail off, and Dani dropped it. She didn't want to argue with him. "Also, for the record, I was not picking her up."

They walked up the gangplank, and a bubble of excitement formed in Dani's chest. She was going on her very first cruise. Probably her only one, and so she needed to forget about her pain and enjoy it.

"Why don't we drop our backpacks off in our rooms and then go get lunch?" Grayson suggested.

They entered the ship and saw that they had to go down four floors to her room. "I don't get lunch on the third deck, remember?"

He frowned. "You're with me. No one will say anything."

She sighed and then gave him a forced grin. All he wanted was for her to be happy, and with all that he was doing for her, it was the least she could do. And she had given him a hard time about that woman. Though that was totally deserved.

"Okay. Shall we check out my room first?" Dani asked, her enthusiasm back. She wanted to see everything on the ship. Grayson said he would stay by her side the whole time, but he had to keep up with her. Once they saw their rooms—and Dani would try not to be jealous of his—they'd go to lunch and then painstakingly check out every nook and cranny they could so that she knew exactly where everything was.

"Sounds like a plan."

They bypassed the elevator and took the stairs instead. They made their way to the end of the ship and into the middle of hundreds of tiny doors. She slid her door key in and froze.

On the bed, there was already a backpack. One that she would recognize anywhere.

"What's the matter?" Grayson poked his head around to see the room.

Her stomach dropped to her knees. "Jeremy's here."

"What?" Grayson looked over her shoulder, his face screwed up in anger. She appreciated his indignation on her part.

"That's his bag." She pointed with a shaky finger.

Grayson sighed and rubbed a hand along his face. "Of all the crappy things he could do. After leaving you at the altar, he decides to take the honeymoon?" Grayson leaned against the wall. The room was so small with both of them in it. Claustrophobia set in, and she felt like she was going to crawl out of her skin. This was absolutely the worst possible thing that could've happened to her. She couldn't quite believe it.

That bubble of excitement burst, and now Dani wanted nothing but to get off the ship. She couldn't spend the next week trying to avoid Jeremy. This was horrible.

But there was still time. She wasn't trapped. Yet.

"I want to go home." She spun around. Grayson crouched so he was at eye level with her.

"No way. This is a huge ship. The odds of running into him are slim at best. And if we do, we'll pretend we are madly in love, and he'll be the one regretting taking the trip. I will not let him ruin this for you." His voice came out harsh and angry.

She shook her head. "I'm supposed to sleep here." She waved at the bed. She wasn't sure how to react. Truthfully she was a little in shock.

"Let's just get you another room. No biggie."

She nodded, at a loss for words. What was Jeremy doing here? Now she'd be looking over her shoulder the whole trip, wondering if Jeremy would be there. She supposed if Grayson were with her, she'd be okay, but if she were alone, she'd go to pieces.

"Come on, let's get out of here. I bet I can even get you an upgrade."

She appreciated his optimism, but she couldn't see how this could possibly turn out okay.

CHAPTER 10

*G*rayson held Dani's trembling hand as they found the elevator and made their way to guest services. She hadn't said a word since they left, and he wasn't sure what she was thinking.

He knew what he was thinking. If he could get Jeremy in a dark corner one night, and the guy fell overboard, he'd never torture Dani again.

He sighed.

That would be too much to wish for.

Grayson hoped that the first time he ran into Jeremy, it was alone and that Dani was off enjoying the spa or something. He wouldn't risk getting detained on the ship, so breaking the bastard's nose was out of the question. His fingers unconsciously clenched into fists.

But he could give him a piece of his mind. He had no idea what the douchebag was doing. Leaving Dani at the altar and taking the honeymoon was lower than low. Maybe taking over Dani's wedding and marrying her wasn't the right thing to do, but over the years, Grayson had just kept quiet when Jeremy did something crappy. And now he was tired of just sitting there and doing nothing. He should've told Dani years ago how he felt. Instead, he was on a cruise with his best friend and ready to commit murder for her.

He had to get his temper in check. He needed to stay positive for Dani and not let her see that this rattled him. Thankfully, he'd been on enough vacations to know that the cruise line would be accommodating.

They found guest services, and Grayson skipped the main line and headed to the suite desk.

A tiny man with a huge mustache stood there. "Ah, Mr. McBride, how can I help you?"

"How did he know your name?" Dani hissed.

"It's my job to know his name," The man said and turned his attention back to Grayson. "Is there a problem with your suite?"

Grayson was still shocked that this man knew exactly who he was, and he hadn't even been on the ship for more than thirty minutes. "What? Oh, no. But

I do have a problem that I hope you'll be able to fix for me."

"I'm sure I can exceed your expectations."

Dani let go of his hand and wandered away to study a picture of a giant fish. She probably didn't want to be around to explain the situation. Grayson didn't blame her.

He dropped his voice. "My friend Dani here is on her honeymoon. But the man she was supposed to marry left her at the altar. I convinced her to take the trip anyway, but so did the douchebag. Can we secure her another room? I'll pay for it."

The man's mustache quivered. "Hm. Let me look."

He typed some things into the computer, and his thick brows furrowed. "I'm sorry. There are no more rooms left. We usually hold back a few in case of problems, but three of our staterooms and one of our suites seem to be having some plumbing issues, so they are all out of order."

Grayson frowned. He would not force Dani to stay with Jeremy, and even if he was okay with it, Dani would bail before the ship left. And she needed this trip. He thought for a second about seeing if he could just book another cruise, but it was too late for that.

"I see. Well, then can you move her to my room?"

They'd figure out the sleeping arrangements later.

This was the best possible scenario. Plus, then he could keep an eye on her.

"Of course. That will be easy." He pushed a few more buttons and handed Grayson a new key with Dani's information and a fancy lanyard.

"Please do enjoy lunch. And if there's anything else we can do to make your stay better, let us know."

Grayson nodded. "Dani," he called.

"Oh, sorry, I got distracted," she said. But he doubted it was the picture that distracted her. He'd bet anything that her mind was on Jeremy and the fear of running into him. Maybe they'd get lucky and never see him.

He handed her the key.

Her eyes lit up. "You got me a new room?"

He liked that he could solve her problems, but she probably wouldn't like the solution.

"Sort of." He rubbed the back of his neck.

"What do you mean 'sort of'?" She asked, warily. He wasn't sure how she'd take this.

"You're staying with me. It's a suite. It will be plenty big enough. There were no other rooms available. They're having plumbing issues, so they had to move some other people into the empty rooms. And the ship is booked full."

Dani swallowed and stared down at her key. "Well, at least that means I'll get lunch in the nice restaurant." Her stomach grumbled, and she chuckled. "That was perfect timing."

"You want to go eat before we find the room?" Grayson could use a bite to eat too. He offered her a hand, and when she took it, he hid his smile. This was where her hand belonged. Not just now, but forever.

CHAPTER 11

*L*unch was totally worth it. The dining room was on an upper deck with views of the water, and the food was to die for. It was almost enough to make Dani forget all about Jeremy and his treachery.

Almost.

"Is this where we'll always eat?" she asked.

Grayson shook his head. "No. I think they only use this for special dinners. I believe there is one on our trip for elite members."

She sighed and stared down at the water. There were some perks to being rich, that was for sure. She worried that she might get used to this and not be able to go back to her poor, sad life.

"Shall we go check out the room?" Grayson asked.

Dani nodded. She didn't know why she was nervous about sharing a room with Grayson. They'd fallen asleep plenty of times together, and it'd never gotten weird. They'd always been just friends, and she liked it that way. Grayson would never break her heart because she'd never let him go beyond just friends.

They gathered their backpacks and headed to Grayson's room. She knew it was her room now too, but that would take some getting used to.

Dani's mouth dropped to the floor. She'd seen pictures of cruise rooms—even suites, and they were all tiny and cramped. This was two floors with a living room, a grand piano, a bar, and three couches.

"This was the small suite?" Dani asked, giving Grayson a look.

He shrugged. "I usually get a level up from this, which has two bedrooms. It's not that much smaller. I can sleep on the couch."

"Don't be stupid. You paid for this. I'll sleep on the couch." She'd have to work for a year just to pay for this.

He took her bag from her and dropped it on a counter. "Nope. We aren't having this conversation."

Dani sighed. "Fine. We'll just sleep in the same bed."

Grayson took a step closer to her, and the heat in

the room suddenly skyrocketed. "Are you sure that's a good idea?"

"Why wouldn't it be?" She didn't like thinking about why. Grayson was her friend. Friends shared beds sometimes.

"I dunno. Because we kissed once. Because you're my wife." He stepped into her personal space.

She rolled her eyes and tried not to think about everything else. "That was all for show. Maybe we should drop the whole wife thing. No one needs to know. Then nothing will get awkward between us."

"What about Jeremy?"

Her stomach fell. She didn't want to think about Jeremy. "You said we won't run into Jeremy. That this is a big ship and I don't have to worry about it."

"You're probably right. I wasn't all that comfortable with the wife stuff anyway. I still get to spoil you though because you are my best friend. You wanna check out the upstairs?"

Dani nodded and raced up the stairs. Now that they were in their room, she was a lot more relaxed. This trip would be amazing, and she would forget all about Jeremy. This would just be like the times she'd gone up to Mackinac with him. A trip between friends.

The bed was in a loft and looked down over the

living room. The view out the window would be amazing when they were out on the water.

She rounded a corner and found a closet that was three times as big as hers at home, and then she squeed when she saw the bathroom.

"I don't ever want to go home," she called to Grayson.

"Why not?"

"Because this bathroom is heaven."

She scrambled into the massive bathtub, which to be fair, was bigger than most hot tubs.

"We don't have to share the hot tubs with creepy old men."

Grayson laughed and climbed in after her. There was no water, but Dani could imagine it.

"Just this creepy old man. Bathing suits are not optional, obviously." He waggled his brows and pretended to leer at her.

She shoved him on the shoulder. "You are not an old man. Creepy maybe, but not old."

"Creepy?" he asked and wiggled his eyebrows.

"Yeah, you married me just so you could kiss me again."

His face fell. "I did that to help you."

She didn't mean to make him feel bad. "I know, and I'm grateful. I'm just teasing you. Thanks for making me come." She sighed and leaned back against the tub.

"I'm glad to see you excited."

"I am." There was horseback riding to look forward to and all the shows.

"You wanna explore the ship?" he asked.

"I don't want to miss disembarking. Can we just chill on the balcony for now?" She was glad she had the view the lady at check-in was talking about so she didn't have to fight for a spot on the eighteenth floor.

"Dani, this is your trip. We can do whatever you want." His face looked so dang sincere.

Her stomach swooped. Jeremy would never say that to her. She often made plans, only to have him change them last minute and not give her a choice in the matter.

Maybe she'd just stay single forever and travel with Grayson. He'd offered before, but she'd always thought it would be weird traveling with both Jeremy and Grayson, so she didn't. But this was the life. She wished she'd done it before now.

Though that would all change when Grayson met his forever. She didn't like thinking about that, and she really didn't like thinking about why she didn't like thinking about that.

CHAPTER 12

a couple of hours later, Dani and Grayson wandered around the ship.

The ship felt packed to the brim with people, but it was incredible. They started at the top and planned to work their way down, checking out everything and taking note of what they wanted to do.

And Dani wanted to do it all, but after the first few floors, her enthusiasm waned. Grayson was sure it was the couples all over the ship. A few women had on honeymoon hats or t-shirts.

Grayson wanted to see her smile again, but he wasn't sure this was the way. They stared at the bumper cars. People were everywhere, and the noise was a little too much for him.

"Come on, Grayson, it will be fun." She smiled, but it was forced.

"I haven't been in a bumper car since I was, like, ten." He didn't know when he became an adult, but somewhere in the last few years, he'd lost his ability to do anything fun. He focused on caring for his loved ones instead and lost himself in his business.

"All the more reason to do it with me." She bumped her hip to his.

Grayson sighed. "Okay, go sign us up."

She squeed and clapped her hands together, and he couldn't help but smile. There was his Dani again.

"Ten o'clock on Tuesday," she said, and they walked past the laser tag room.

"That's what I want to do." He waved at the sign. He loved anything competitive, and he was pretty good at laser tag.

"I suck at laser tag." She pouted, and all he could think about was that he wanted to kiss those lips again. Maybe in a dark corner of the laser tag room.

"I know. That's why I want to do it."

"Maybe later," she said and dragged him away. Somehow, they ended up in the library, which had no one in it. Grayson wondered what it must've been like in the old cruising days when one of the best things about the ship was relaxing on the deck with a book.

Dani perused a shelf, and he stood close enough

that he could smell her honeysuckle shampoo. He wasn't sure how he would get through this week without kissing her again. He kept reliving it in his head. It was the moment he'd dreamed about for years, and now she just thought it was all fake. She'd made it very clear that she wanted him to stay in the friendzone. But he'd married her. He couldn't just keep her at a distance. He wanted so much more. He'd never force that on her, of course, but he wished he knew why she'd never given him a chance.

A couple of giggles made both Grayson and Dani turn their heads. A young couple tumbled into the room, hands everywhere on each other. The guy pushed the girl against a bookshelf and shoved his tongue down her throat.

Dani looked up at Grayson, and he winked at her. "I'm sure you have a room," he said, keeping his voice light.

The couple extracted their lips from one another but with zero bashfulness.

"Oh, sorry," the girl said with a giggle. "It's our honeymoon."

Grayson almost said, "Ours too," but then remembered that Dani told him they should just act like friends. "Well, have fun. We'll go find another place to talk."

He placed a hand on Dani's back and led her out of

the room. But they hadn't walked ten feet before they turned a corner and ran into another couple making out.

They passed them, and when they were out of earshot, Dani chuckled. "I guess this is the make-out floor."

"I guess it is."

And we should join them. But he didn't say it aloud.

They entered the casino, and while there wasn't anyone making out, not a soul was in there by themselves. Couples were everywhere. Though he supposed people probably thought he and Dani were one too.

They exited the other side and strode into the solarium. It was one of the few adult-only spots on the boat. A few people swam in the pool, and Dani sat down and put her feet in the water. Grayson joined her.

"Okay, so this is going to be a good week," she said, smiling.

"The best," he replied. *Mostly because I'm with you.*

She laid her head on his shoulder. "Thanks for being so good to me. I don't know what I would do without you."

He put his arm around her waist and pulled her close to him. "That goes both ways. Don't forget that you've been there when I've needed you too."

"Not as well as I should've because sometimes Jeremy was jealous. I'm sorry that when your sister died, I wasn't around that much."

"That's okay. I didn't really want people around." He didn't like talking about when his sister died, and Dani had been way more supportive than she thought. It was several years ago, but it still pained him. She got cancer, and he couldn't fix it. He liked fixing problems for the people he loved, and this was something neither he nor her husband could do anything about. Tristan had moved on, and Grayson was happy for him, but her loss still hit Grayson hard. He didn't like thinking about it.

A young woman in a white string bikini climbed down the stairs next to him and slid into the water. She was the kind of woman he'd find attractive if Dani weren't around. But lately, all his thoughts were with her.

A man on the other side of the pool smiled as she swam closer, but he made no move to approach her. She, however, swam up to him, wrapped her arms around him, and planted a kiss on his lips.

Dani busted out laughing. "I think we need to find another floor."

"How about the bar?" Grayson asked.

"That sounds perfect. I need to find myself a pina colada."

CHAPTER 13

*D*ani ran back to the room to change her shorts since they'd gotten wet by the pool. She enjoyed exploring the boat with Grayson, but all the kissing couples made her uncomfortable. She'd picked this cruise because it seemed like it was the most romantic, but that didn't bode well for her now. She should be the one kissing her new husband, but instead, she was busy trying not to have feelings for him.

It would be so easy to give in and just pretend they were a couple on the boat. Kiss and even sleep together, but she knew the second they arrived home, he'd drop her. Because men like Grayson didn't stay with girls like her. Not that Grayson was a user. It was just that she was always the leftover girl and

Grayson deserved someone better than that. And if she allowed herself to pretend, even for the week, after it was over, she'd be out a best friend.

Grayson said he'd meet her at the pool bar and order her pina colada. She often wondered why he was her friend. He was so good to her all the time. Something about them just clicked, and things were easy. Like a brother and sister. As long as she kept it that way, she'd prevent her heart from getting broken.

It only took her a few minutes to change, but she got distracted by the view off the balcony. She could probably be just as happy never leaving the room, but she'd also know what she was missing. There was way too much to do on the boat.

On the way back, she dodged several kids with ice cream dripping down their arms, the cones practically mushed in their hands. She expected that more than once on a boat like this. Unsuspecting adults got ice cream on their pants because some kid was careless. It was the kind of thing Grayson would laugh about, but Jeremy would get angry and probably make the kid cry.

She wondered, now that things were over with Jeremy, whether she'd be able to find someone who did want kids. It was the one thing she'd always wished Jeremy would've given her. But he absolutely refused to even talk about having kids.

She made her way onto the pool deck, which had many more families and not a single kissing couple. This was much better. She could hang out with the kids and not feel like she was supposed to be on the most romantic vacation of her life.

The bar area was packed with girls in teeny bikinis and men in swim trunks. Maybe she should've just put her suit on.

She spotted Grayson on the other side, surrounded by women who looked way better in their bikinis than she would in hers.

She approached, and Grayson's eyes lit up. "Dani, come meet my new friends." He handed her a pina colada, and she sipped at the cool slush. She wondered how many more of them it would take for her to forget about Jeremy.

Grayson pulled her toward him, placing a hand on her back. "This is Sara, Michelle, and Barbie."

Barbie looked like her namesake with big boobs and a tiny waist. The others were just as pretty, and none of their bikinis covered up what they should. Normally, she wouldn't judge, but she didn't like Grayson looking at them.

Which was stupid because Grayson wasn't even hers, and he never would be.

Dani forced a smile. "Nice to meet you."

Sara gave a sympathetic smile and placed a hand

on Dani's arm. "Grayson told us all what happened to you, and we're so sorry. It was so good of him to step up and help you like that. I wish I had someone like him."

"I bet you do," Dani said with false enthusiasm. Inside, she was grumbling. She wanted to hang out with him alone, not with other people. And she had no idea why he would share their story with these women. She shouldn't be jealous, but then again, if Grayson ran off with one of these women, then he wouldn't be able to be there for her this trip. It wasn't that she thought he should be with her instead. At least, she didn't think so. But she also didn't know why he would tell these women her story.

"Yeah, Grayson told us he'd pay for a spa day for all of us, so you can get some girl time," Michelle said. Ah. He was trying to make her friends. That she didn't want. But also, he was blind if he thought they were going to be there for her. They wanted him.

"Not me," Barbie said, batting her eyes at Grayson. "I'm going to stay and keep Grayson entertained." She leaned closer to him, her boobs resting on his arm. Dani resisted the urge to roll her eyes.

"While it was nice to meet you all, I prefer spa days alone, not with others. And, Grayson, it's time to get ready for dinner." She wasn't trying to be possessive, but she had to get him away from these girls, or she'd lose him for the whole trip.

Grayson nodded and grabbed his drink, standing. Barbie leaned up and gave him a sloppy kiss on the cheek. "Meet me back here after dinner."

Grayson smiled and moved toward Dani. "Nice to meet you, ladies. We'll see you later."

"After dinner," Barbie called, wiggling her fingers toward him. Ugh.

Dani fumed all the way to the room. She flung the door open and stomped in. She wasn't doing a good job keeping her temper in check.

"Are you mad at me?" Grayson asked, his brow furrowed.

"Yes," Dani replied before she could stop herself.

He creased his eyebrows. "Why?"

She gripped her glass harder. She couldn't explain to him that she was jealous. "Because what if Jeremy saw you? Then he'd know I was just here as a pity date, not a real bride. Or he'd think that you were more of an asshole than he was."

Grayson's face softened, and he approached her. He extracted her drink from her and held tight to both of her hands.

"I'm very sorry. I didn't think about that. You'd said you didn't want to pretend that we're husband

and wife. They blindsided me, and I told them I was here with my friend."

Dani swallowed. Grayson was doing this for her, and she was making it harder for him. She just worried that if they continued to play pretend, then she might forget it wasn't real.

"I know. Maybe I was wrong. We can't risk Jeremy finding out it was fake."

Grayson nodded. "Okay. Then we need to introduce each other as husband and wife. We don't need to be all over each other, but if I had said I was waiting for my wife, those women would've left me alone."

Dani grinned. "That's debatable, but they certainly would've fled when I arrived."

"So, wife again?" he asked with some trepidation.

"I think so." That's the only way she was going to get through this week, but she was still scared of what would happen when it was over.

"Then it's settled. Let's go to dinner and make some couple friends." He took the stairs up to the bedroom two at a time, and she watched his back.

Maybe this was a bad idea after all.

She should've just stayed home.

CHAPTER 14

ani was giving Grayson emotional whiplash. But he wasn't going to lie. Seeing her all jealous like that made his heart soar. She might've said it was because she didn't want to risk Jeremy seeing them, but he saw right through that. She wanted him, and that was something he could work with.

Maybe he should fake picking up girls at a bar more often. Dani was far better company, but he had been bored and said more than he should've. Women were always easy to talk to. But he had no desire to do anything with them.

He showered first and then waited for Dani on the balcony. He didn't dress up, but he put on slacks instead of shorts and a button-down short-sleeve shirt.

One of his favorite things to do on a cruise was to watch the waves. He could stare at them for hours. After his sister died, he'd taken a trip where he literally did just that. Stared at the waves the whole time.

The balcony door opened, and Grayson spun around. Dani stood there with her hair twisted up, in a pretty blue sundress that showed off her bronzed skin and curves. Grayson swallowed. Unlike the women at the bar, keeping his hands off of her would be a challenge.

"You look gorgeous," he said.

Dani blushed. "Thanks. You clean up pretty good yourself."

"Shall we?" he asked.

She nodded, and they left the room. Grayson wasn't sure what to do at this point. Should he try to hold her hand or not? If they saw Jeremy, he definitely would. Would it look weird if people saw them and they weren't holding hands? Lots of couples didn't hold hands. He wasn't sure how to do this fake thing.

"I've heard the food on cruise ships is to die for. Lunch was good, but that was just for Elite members, so I'm worried this won't measure up," Dani said.

"Food is hit and miss. I personally enjoy the social

aspect of it better. If you have a good group at your table, you can make decent friends."

They turned a corner, and Dani stopped dead. "What's the matter?" Grayson asked.

She slid her arm around his waist. "It's Jeremy," she hissed.

Grayson jerked his head up. Sure enough, Jeremy headed in their direction, a drink in his hand. Grayson hadn't expected to run into him so soon. He had hoped, for Dani's sake, that they didn't. But here they were.

Jeremy's face lit up when he laid eyes on Dani, but then it turned to a scowl as he saw Grayson. The nerve of that guy. Grayson had half a mind to punch him right in the nose.

"Dani," he called, and her grip on Grayson's shirt tightened. He let his arm rest on her shoulders, her skin warm on his.

"What are you doing here?" Dani said as Jeremy closed the distance.

"We booked this trip six months ago. Why wouldn't I come?" He said it all so nonchalantly, like he couldn't figure out what the big deal was. What an idiot.

"Because it was supposed to be our honeymoon," Dani said, her voice coming out in a shriek. Grayson couldn't believe the audacity of this guy. He knew that

Dani would want to fight her own battles, so he kept his mouth shut, but he'd intervene if he had to. For now, he kept her close.

Jeremy pursed his lips. "You know I didn't want to get married. But that doesn't mean our relationship is over. I waited in our room for a bit for you, but you never showed. Looks like you're ready for dinner though."

Grayson waited for Dani to retort, but Jeremy seemed to have left her speechless.

Time to intervene. "I don't know what planet you come from, but here on earth, when you leave someone at the altar, the relationship is over."

Jeremy clenched his fists. "I know you and Dani are close, but you've always been jealous of our relationship. You don't understand what Dani and I have. She and I will always be together. Marriage doesn't change that."

Jeremy reached for Dani's hand, and Grayson had enough. He grabbed Jeremy's hand and jerked him away from Dani. Jeremy dropped his drink as Grayson shoved him up against the wall.

"Jealous? Hardly. The second you left her, she fell right into my arms. We've been in love for years right under your nose, and you had no idea. Just in case you haven't heard the news, she's my wife now, so don't you ever touch her again."

He let go of Jeremy and turned to Dani. "Let's go," he said, holding out his hand.

For half a second he thought she wasn't going to take it, but her small hand slid into his, and they left Jeremy sputtering in the hallway. Once they were out of earshot, Grayson slowed down. "Are you okay?"

Dani nodded. "I didn't expect him to be like that."

"You mean to act as if your relationship hadn't changed a bit? He left you at the altar." Grayson wasn't sure what on earth Jeremy was thinking.

"Yeah. Thank you for sticking up for me." She seemed relieved.

"That's what husbands do. From here on out, I'm your shield from Jeremy and your excuse if you don't want to hang out with anyone else."

She chuckled, leaning into him. "You definitely have your advantages."

He tugged her a little closer. "We don't have to go to dinner if you don't want to. We can totally go back to the room and order in."

He kind of hoped she would. He didn't feel like meeting other people tonight. He was fuming over Jeremy, and he just wanted to be alone with her.

She shook her head. "No way. This will likely be the only cruise I take in my life, and I want to make sure I experience it all."

CHAPTER 15

*D*ani was still rattled when they entered the dining room. A part of her loved Jeremy and probably always would. He was safe, and she wasn't sure she was worthy of anyone better than him.

She'd love to be with a guy like Grayson, but he was way out of her league. He was smart and well-educated. Good-looking and nice in a way that most guys weren't.

Dani was a college dropout, slightly overweight, and not exactly pretty in the traditional sense. Even though Jeremy had been to vet school and had a good job, he still loved her, and she'd never figured that out. He was smart, and she wasn't. Something that Jeremy reminded her of quite often. How lucky her fat ass was to be with him. And he was right. She was lucky he'd chosen her. Though he had his faults as well, which was why she knew Jeremy was right for her. He had a quick temper and was slightly balding. He was demanding in a way most men weren't.

But she knew she wasn't worthy of anyone better. This was the best she was going to get. Her father's voice played in her ears. *Unless you lose that weight, no boy is ever going to like you, you dumb bitch.*

She shook her head. She hadn't thought of her father in years. Though the rejection from Jeremy was probably triggering it.

She squeezed Grayson's hand tighter and refocused her thoughts. This trip with her best friend would be amazing. She needed alcohol.

Grayson followed the waiter to their table, and he seated them with two other couples. One set of chairs was left.

The woman to her right waved. "Hi. I'm Jenny. Mike and I are on our honeymoon. So are Tasha and Dean." She pointed to the other couple. Grayson rested his arm along the back of her chair, and she wanted to lean into it.

"So are we," he said.

Jenny squealed and clapped her hands. "Oh, that's so awesome. We're the honeymoon table." She danced in her seat. Dani wasn't sure if she'd like Jenny or not.

She was very excitable, but that energy could be contagious.

Someone knocked into Dani's chair and shoved her into the table. Grayson pulled her close to him, and she could smell his faint cologne that she always associated with being safe.

Dani jerked around. The couple from the library stood behind her, their lips locked once again. Dani nearly rolled her eyes.

The woman extracted herself. "Oh, sorry. We get a little carried away," she said and dropped into the chair next to Dani. The guy sat next to her and scooted his chair as close as he could get to her and then stuck his tongue down her throat again. Dani didn't know if she'd be able to take this.

Jenny giggled. "Definitely honeymooners."

The woman finally came up for air, and Dani wondered if she'd ever been that lovesick before. Certainly not with Jeremy.

The woman giggled. "Sorry. Well, not really. We can't keep our hands off of each other. We're just so thrilled to be married. I'm Sonya, and this is Steve."

Everyone else introduced themselves, and then orders were taken. Dani tried to ignore the slurping sounds next to her. She scooted as close as she could to Grayson.

"So, this is so exciting that we all just got married.

Maybe we should tell the stories of how we met and stuff. We can each take a different night," Jenny said.

Maybe Dani and Grayson would eat alone after this. She couldn't hack all this romance stuff.

Sonya plucked a strawberry out of a bowl in front of her and fed it to Steve. "Oh, I love that idea. Can we go first?"

"If you can keep your lips off of each other long enough," Dani muttered without pausing to think about it.

Sonya giggled and shoved her on the shoulder. "Oh, you're so funny."

"Go on." Jenny dug into her salad. "Let's hear it."

"Well," Sonya began, but then started giggling because Steve kissed her neck. "Stop," she said. "I'll never get the story told if you keep kissing me."

He tugged her closer. "I don't care if the story gets told. I can't keep my lips off of you." He planted his lips on her again.

Dani practically gagged into her drink but kept it together. Grayson seemed unperturbed, but he was good at masking his true emotions.

"Okay, so let me try again," She said with a giggle as Steve sucked on her neck. "Last week, I was work-ing, and Steve came in."

"What do you do?" Dani asked.

"I'm a waitress at IHOP. Steve is a truck driver.

Anyway. He comes in and orders, like, four different breakfasts. I thought it was kind of odd, but I didn't say anything."

"Did you say last week?" Jenny asked. "This is supposed to be about how you met."

"Yeah. Last week. Anyway, I bring him his food, and he stares at all of it and finally says, 'I can't eat all of this. Will you join me?' I was working, so you know, I couldn't, but it was time for my break, so I sat next to him and told him how tired I was because I'd been working all night. So he told me to rest my little hands and fed me breakfast. Isn't that the most romantic thing ever?"

Dani didn't respond, and the rest of the table went quiet. No one knew what to make of such a ridiculous story. She wondered if it would even last.

"That sure is," Grayson said, keeping his voice even. Dani wondered if he was trying not to laugh. "But that was a week ago. How did you get here?" Grayson was always good at making absurd situations seem normal.

"Oh, well. I told him that no one has ever done anything like that for me before, and he said that was a shame and that I deserved to have someone take care of me. Then he asked me to marry him, and I said yes. Here we are." She giggled again, and Steve gave her a sloppy kiss.

Jenny swallowed and smoothed down her hair. Dani doubted that was the kind of story she was looking for.

"That was a delightful story," Jenny said. "Dani, you get to go tomorrow night."

Dani nodded but didn't respond. She and Grayson would talk about it later.

The story may have been ridiculous, but it made her forget all about Jeremy.

CHAPTER 16

*D*inner was an exercise in patience. The couples were all sickening in love, and even though none were as affectionate as Sonya and Steve, Grayson was ready to call it a night before dessert arrived.

But Dani never missed dessert, so he stuck it out.

The one good thing was that Dani was so eager to get away from Sonya and Steve that she was practically in his lap the whole meal. He'd never been in a relationship like Sonya and Steve's before. Though if he did finally manage to land Dani, he hoped they'd be just as annoyingly affectionate in public.

"Oooh, I have an idea," Sonya crowed just as the desserts arrived. Grayson got cheesecake with a strawberry glaze, and Dani went for the massive chocolate cake. Her eyes widened when they set it in front of her.

"I can't eat all that," she said.

"Don't worry. I'll help," Grayson said with a wink. Dani had a thing about wasting food, and even when he'd taken her out to dinner, she always ordered small portions and ate every bite.

Dani picked up her fork, but Sonya snatched it away. "Wait, you haven't heard my idea." Dani glared at her but didn't say anything.

"Go on then," Jenny said. "What's your idea."

"I think all the women should rest their pretty hands and let the husbands feed them dessert."

Jenny nodded. "That sounds terribly romantic." Tasha readily agreed.

Before Dani could argue, Grayson extracted Dani's fork from Sonya's hand. "I agree," he said. He didn't want Dani to feel like she was any less loved than any of the other women at the table. They had a ruse to keep up, and he planned to do just that.

"You don't have to do this," Dani hiss quietly.

"Yes, I do." He eyed all the other couples at the table who were fixated on their new spouses, and slid the fork through the cake and held it up.

Dani let out a breath and opened her mouth, and he slid the fork inside. Dani closed her eyes and moaned a little. "That is divine," she said.

Grayson cleared his throat. "Glad you think so." He had to keep his hormones in check.

Dani opened her eyes and looked at him, her cheeks flushed, and he fed her another bite. She leaned closer to him and rested her fingers lightly on his thigh.

Get a grip on yourself. What he wanted to do was kiss those chocolaty lips of hers, but for her, this wasn't real, and he'd likely get a slap to the face. Instead, he continued to feed her and ignore his growing need. He'd managed to do it for ten years, and he didn't know why it was harder now.

Yes, he did. It was because she was now his wife, and he wanted to keep it that way.

Dani was only able to eat half of the cake, and he finished off the rest, not bothering with his own. Feeding her was strangely intimate. More so than they'd ever been before.

He stood and offered Dani his hand. She took it and leaned into him as they made their way back to the room. Maybe she felt the tension as much as he did. But he wasn't sure if she'd act on it or even let him. He didn't want to push her.

"So, Sonya and Steve are something else, huh?" she asked.

Grayson chuckled. "That's one way to put it. My money's on them not even speaking by the end of the cruise. Couples that act like that burn out way fast."

She shoved against him. "Oh, don't be like that. I think it's romantic, though I could do with a little less make-out time at the table." She hesitated before continuing. "Have you ever been with someone like that?"

"Like what?" he asked, his mind still back at the table feeding her cake.

"You know, someone you were so enamored with that you couldn't keep your hands off of each other, even in public."

"No." Though he wondered, if he and Dani ever moved into that phase, whether they would. Maybe for a while. They had ten years of denial to make up for.

"Me neither. In some ways, I kind of envy them. I mean it's nauseating, but can you imagine being so in love that you don't care what anyone thinks?"

Grayson slid the keycard into the door and pushed it open. Dani had been much freer with her affection since dinner started, and Grayson wasn't sure he could stand it. If he took things the wrong way and read more into it than he should, he could end up making a massive mistake if she withdrew.

Dani turned, rose up on her tiptoes, and placed a soft kiss on his cheek. "Thanks for an amazing night," she whispered, her body pressed into his. "And thanks for being such a good friend." She stepped away from him.

"I think I'm going to head to the gym," he said. *Friend* was not a word he wanted to hear tonight, and it was obvious she still had him firmly in that zone.

"Why? I thought we'd watch the sunset." She waved to the balcony doors where the sun was sinking into the water.

"Maybe tomorrow night. I'll be back in a bit." He didn't want things to get out of control and have something happen that couldn't be taken back.

He raced upstairs and changed into his gym clothes, opting for loose basketball shorts, and slid out the door. Dani was already on the balcony.

He had to get ahold of himself, or he might do something he'd regret.

And he couldn't risk any regrets with Dani.

CHAPTER 17

The sun sank deep into the water, and Dani watched it go all the way. She was a little irked that Grayson just disappeared. The night had been incredible, and she wasn't ready for it to end.

And the thing that made the night amazing was Grayson. Serious sparks had been flying between them, and on more than one occasion, Dani thought Grayson might kiss her, but he never did.

Which was probably for the best. She wasn't sure their friendship could handle a fling in the middle of it. If she was being honest with herself, she wasn't sure she'd recover from something like that.

No one made her feel special like Grayson did.

And once they crossed that line, she'd want it forever.

Which she'd never have because men like Grayson didn't stay with women like her.

Once darkness fell, Dani didn't see the point in sitting outside by herself. But she didn't know what to do. Staying in the room watching television seemed a stupid waste of time on a cruise.

She wanted Grayson to come back.

She picked up the daily itinerary and scanned through the evening activities. It was too late to hit a show, but there was a wine tasting in the piano bar that started in fifteen minutes. That was right up her alley. She didn't know how long Grayson would be, but she wasn't about to miss out on something fun because he was a party pooper.

She left a quick note and then made her way to the bar. She was a few minutes early, but she saw the sommelier setting up. She found a stool at an empty table and sat, waiting. There were a few others there, all couples.

"You know, I've never liked that dress. Perhaps we should go back to our room and take it off."

She spun, nearly falling off the stool. "Jeremy, what are you doing here?" She swallowed down the panic. She had no idea what to say or do. She hated this. This was why she shouldn't have left the room without Grayson.

Jeremy hoisted himself onto the stool next to her. "The same thing you are, I imagine." He waved his hand toward the wine.

She grabbed her purse, ready to make a run for it. A little wine wasn't worth an evening with Jeremy. She could probably talk Grayson into having a private wine tasting in their room.

Jeremy grabbed her hand. "No, wait. I wanted to talk to you without that bastard around."

Dani bristled. "He's not the one who left me at the altar."

The nerve Jeremy had, accosting her like this.

Something changed behind Jeremy's eyes. "I'm sorry. I panicked at the wedding, and I really want to explain myself." He ran a hand through his hair. She supposed she owed him the opportunity. Plus, she kind of wanted to hear his reasoning. "It was all those people, and you were so excited, and all I could think about was how much I didn't want to get married."

That was a weak argument. "That's supposed to make me feel better? I was ready to commit to you for the rest of our lives, and you left me there. You could've at least given me the courtesy of doing it before the wedding."

Jeremy rolled his eyes. "We both know that marriage vows mean nothing anymore. As far as I'm concerned, there is no one else. You know that. It's you and me until we die. But I can't get married. I'm sorry. We can do all the other things. Have kids, buy a house, go on vacations together. But I just can't do marriage. Please don't leave me. I love you, and I'll never stop loving you. We were made for each other."

Dani was shocked that he brought up kids. He'd always been a firm no on them, but now they were back on the table. He'd give her kids but not a marriage. The look in his eyes was almost enough for Dani to falter. But then she closed her eyes and remembered the way she felt when he left her all alone. That wasn't forgivable. She extracted her hand from under his and slid off the stool.

"Actions speak louder than words. And thankfully, I've found someone who does love me enough to marry me. You're too late, Jeremy. I'm already taken."

Jeremy glowered at her. "It's never gonna last. Grayson just knew that was the best way to get into your pants. Men like him don't stay with women like you, Dani, and you're delusional if you think he will. Open your eyes, and come back to me before I realize how much better off I am without you as well."

Tears pricked Dani's eyes, and she rushed from the room. She'd really thought she'd gotten the better of Jeremy, but in the end, it was him that got to her.

She wasn't worthy of a man like Grayson, which was why the wedding was a sham to begin with.

Maybe she should go back to Jeremy before it was too late.

CHAPTER 18

"*L*et's go swimming," Grayson said. Dani had been sitting out on the balcony all morning, pouting. When he got back to the room after the gym, he'd found her in bed, crying.

After she told him what happened, he wanted to hunt Jeremy down. But he didn't because he didn't want to leave Dani alone. He'd held her while she cried herself to sleep, but she was still off this morning.

Dani had always had low self-esteem. Her no-good father had always talked down to her and told her how worthless she was. And as many times as Grayson had tried to tell her otherwise, she just didn't believe it.

Now Jeremy was doing the same thing.

"How do we handle Jeremy now?" she asked, not making eye contact.

"We'll just give him a show and make him see how much better off you are with me instead of him." He wasn't going to lie, he would enjoy that probably way more than he should.

She stretched her legs out long, and Grayson resisted the urge to lay his hand on her thigh. His hormones weren't making this any easier.

"I don't know. I'm enjoying just watching the sea."

Time to be a hardass. She'd appreciate it in the end. "No. You're moping. That's not allowed on this trip. Now come on. Go put on your skimpiest bikini, and let's go sit by the pool. If Jeremy shows up, he'll see exactly what he's missing out on."

He wasn't going to lie. He wanted to see Dani in a skimpy bikini as well. They'd gone swimming before, but she'd always worn a one-piece. When she'd put her clothes away in the closet, he'd spied a couple of string bikinis. And this was a good excuse to get her into one.

She leveled a look at him. "Fine. But only if you promise me another pina colada."

Finally, she was seeing some sense.

"You can have as many as you want." He dragged her up the stairs, grabbed his suit out of the closet, and changed in the other bathroom while she took the big one.

He didn't bother putting a shirt on. Dani came out of the bathroom with a cover-up over whatever suit she put on, and Grayson was a little disappointed because it covered up way too much.

They headed up to the pool, found a couple of chairs, and Dani dropped into one.

"I'll go get us drinks," he said. He made his way around the pool to the bar. He ordered a pina colada for Dani and a beer for himself. He didn't need anything stronger at the moment.

"You know, I always knew you had a thing for her. I guess I can wait until you're done with her, but I don't like it. Why don't you save us both a little heartache and give her back?"

Grayson spun around to face the S.O.B. next to him. He had been waiting for time alone with Jeremy so he could give the guy a piece of his mind.

"I never figured out what she was doing with a loser like you. I was just biding my time until you screwed up. Because I tell you this, now that I have her, I'm never letting her go."

Grayson grabbed the drinks and made his way back to Dani. He didn't need to hear anything else Jeremy had to say.

Dani had taken off the cover-up and sat there in a

teeny white bikini. His heart raced, but he couldn't let her see how she affected him. Not now with Jeremy so close. Plus, he didn't want to spook her.

He sat down on his lounge chair and handed Dani her drink.

"Don't look, but your douchebag is at the bar."

Dani paled and took a sip of her pina colada. "I told you," she hissed. "We should've stayed in the room.

"And I told you, we'll just make him jealous."

Dani rolled her eyes. "And how will we do that?"

"Make out by the pool?"

"Don't be silly," Dani said, blushing.

"Oh, come on. You and I both know that it will make him see red." He wanted to kiss Dani, but this wasn't about that. He really wanted to make Jeremy see that Dani was worth more than the likes of him.

She eyed Grayson again. "Are you sure?"

"I am. We've already kissed once. Another one won't hurt anything."

The resolve in her face told him he'd won, and he leaned over to kiss her, but she surprised him by pushing him away and climbing out of her chair.

She set down her drink, extracted his from his hand, and climbed onto his lap.

Holy hell, this was hot. He was not expecting her to be so bold. She straddled him, placing her hands on his chest, and stared deep into his eyes, a question hanging between them.

He set his hands on her hips, his fingers brushing the bare skin of her back. He wasn't sure what was happening here, but he knew he'd never recover. This was the moment he'd been dreaming about for years.

She leaned over and whispered in his ear. "Is he watching?" she asked, her voice breathless.

Grayson stole a quick glance at the bar, having completely forgotten about Jeremy. He was indeed watching them, a scowl on his face.

"He is," Grayson said.

"Well, then let's give him a show he'll never forget."

Then she leaned over and pressed her lips against his.

CHAPTER 19

*D*ani had no idea what possessed her to be so bold, but she felt sexy in her skimpy bikini and was tired of hiding from Jeremy. Plus, for just one moment, she wanted to know what it was like to be with someone like Grayson. She could pretend here out on the pool deck because things wouldn't go too far.

She leaned into Grayson, deepening the kiss, sliding her hands into his hair. His fingers dug into her hips, and he teased her lips with his tongue. She let him in, all thought disappearing.

Right now, this wasn't her best friend. This was the kiss she'd always dreamed of. It was a moment she'd never forget. And she'd treasure it because it was the only one she was going to get.

After a few seconds, or maybe it was eons, she pulled away, but instead of letting her go, Grayson leaned forward and kissed her neck, trailing kisses to her ear.

"Maybe we should go back to our room," he whispered, and the spell broke. She jerked away.

"Or maybe we should cool off in the pool." She didn't want him to think she was upset by his suggestion, so she winked and gave him another soft kiss. Then she climbed off him and jumped into the deep end of the pool.

She knew that he was just like any other man, driven by lust, and that, if he did sleep with her, he'd regret it the next day because he wouldn't want her again. She loved him too much to let this get in the way. She needed him, and she couldn't let her own feelings muddy the water.

She came up out of the water and caught the tail end of Grayson yelling cannonball, and he drenched her.

She laughed and splashed him when he came up. He grabbed her and pulled her under the water.

This was what friends did, and she was grateful for him. He made sure things never got awkward.

They played in the water for a bit and then hovered around the shallow end.

"What do you want to do the rest of the day?"

Grayson asked, his eyes taking her in, in ways they'd never done before. She couldn't let him do this as much as she wanted to. They had to stay out in public until he saw her as just his friend again.

"I dunno. We're already soaked. We can check out the waterslide maybe."

"Sounds like a plan." He got out and offered her his hand. She took it and climbed out after him. He handed her a towel and dried off his hair, and Dani slipped on her cover-up. They walked across the deck and past the bar. Jeremy was nowhere in sight.

"Oh, ice cream," Dani said, spotting a self-serve machine.

She made Grayson a cone and then one for herself. It was hot outside, and they immediately started melting. Grayson licked the ice cream off of his hand, and all Dani could think about was how much she wanted him to do the same to her.

Get a hold of yourself, girl. She let out a breath.

They walked up to the waterslide, eating their ice cream in silence, and she wondered briefly if Grayson was thinking about the kiss but didn't want to ask him and make it all awkward because then he might suggest they go back to the room again.

The line for the waterslide was long and hot.

"What will we say when Jenny asks for our love story tonight?" Dani asked, fanning her face.

"The truth."

"And what exactly is that?"

"That we've been in love for years but just never admitted it because of Jeremy. And when he left you at the altar, I confessed my feelings for you, and we got married. Now we regret all those years we lost."

Dani nodded. "I certainly regret all those years I gave to Jeremy." And she did. She would've been better off single. Then her heart wouldn't be broken right now.

"Well, at least, you found out before you got married. It's a whole lot easier to get out before the papers are signed."

The line moved, and they could now see several people lined up on the stairs beneath them. The higher they got, the better the view got. This was their first sea day. Tomorrow they'd be in Jamaica, and Dani couldn't wait. She had a whole day planned out. Sure, she'd thought she was going to be on a romantic day with Jeremy, but it'd still be fun with Grayson.

"True."

But still. She wasted eight years of her life on Jeremy, and now she had nothing to show for it.

CHAPTER 20

*G*rayson knew the kiss the day before was just to make Jeremy jealous, but he couldn't stop thinking about it. In fact, he'd barely slept the night before. Dani was just inches from him, and he couldn't have her, not like he wanted to.

She'd blown him off when he suggested they head back to the room, so it must not have had the same effect on her as it did him. He'd hoped that he'd cool off during the day, but his desire for her had only grown.

"What's on the plan today?" Grayson asked. They were eating breakfast on the balcony, watching the hustle and bustle of the dock. They'd arrived in Jamaica overnight, and she'd already been down to the excursion desk to switch it over from her and Jeremy to her and Grayson.

"Horseback riding in the ocean, a tour of a sugar plantation, and then a dinner cruise."

"Sounds fun." He wondered if maybe she'd let her guard down and kiss him again. He had to wait for her to make the first move, but he could certainly encourage it.

"I can't wait." She practically bounced in her seat.

They finished eating and headed down to the docks. They approached the meeting place for the excursion and heard a loud squeal.

Jenny raced up to meet them. "Oh, you're here. Yay! Our whole table signed up for the honeymooner's day."

Grayson eyed Dani. "The honeymooner's day?"

She sighed. "Yeah. Sorry. I wanted to do the horseback riding, so I figured why not?"

Jenny didn't seem to be listening to anything that Dani said. She just clapped her hands and squealed again. "It's going to be so romantic. The sunset cruise with dancing and champagne."

Dani just shrugged, and Grayson put an arm around her shoulder. They had to make it look like they were in love. He wanted her close.

They chatted with the other couples for a bit, and

then a very lively Jamaican man called them to attention and started explaining the trip. Grayson and Dani stood near the back of the crowd.

"Hey, Dani," someone said, and Dani jerked around. Grayson glanced over.

"What are you doing here?" she asked, and Jeremy just smirked. Grayson couldn't believe the nerve of that guy.

"I could ask you the same thing. Last I checked. I paid for this excursion." He glanced up at Grayson with a scowl.

"It's my honeymoon. You left me at the altar." Her words came out in a squeak.

Dani's day would be completely ruined if Jeremy tagged along.

"Look, man, I'll pay you back for the whole thing. Just leave us alone," Grayson said, tugging Dani closer to him.

"It's not money I want. It's Dani."

"Then maybe you should've married her." Grayson was so over this guy. He and Dani should've booked a different cruise.

"Whatever. I'm going on this trip, and you can't stop me."

He weaved his way through the crowd to check in with the host.

Grayson was not letting this happen. He wasn't spending the whole day with that prick. "We can bail. I'll find a private tour company to do everything you wanted to."

Dani shook her head. "It's okay."

"Is it the money? Because we talked about that. You have to let me spoil you. And Jeremy on this tour will ruin it for you. I just want you to be happy."

She let out a sigh. "I know, but I can't let him run me away from things. I have to work with him, for goodness sake. How will I do that if I can't spend a day on the same tour as him?"

Grayson nodded. He understood her logic, but he didn't like it. Jeremy was proving to be more of a nuisance than he'd originally thought.

"Okay. We'll stay away from him. But also. When we get home, I'm finding you a new job."

"I like my job," she said. "You can't just boss me around like that."

He let out a breath. Sometimes his temper got away from him. "I know. But there is more than one vet's office. What I meant was that I could help you find a new one so you don't have to work for him anymore."

Dani gave a stiff nod. They would have to fix that later. For now, he'd focus on making sure Jeremy didn't ruin her day.

The tour guide left to find the bus, and Jeremy chatted with Sonya and Steve, glancing up at Dani from time to time.

"Do you want me to kiss you again?" Grayson asked.

"No," she said with a little more force than he thought was necessary.

"Sorry. I didn't realize it upset you that much last time. I won't do it again." His emotion was already running a little high. He knew it came out angry, but Jeremy was getting under his skin.

"Grayson, it's not that." Her eyes pleaded with him.

"Don't worry about it. Seriously. I'm going to go talk to Dean and Mike." His temper was running a little high, and he didn't want to take it out on her.

He left her behind with Jenny and Tasha. He didn't want her to see that she'd hurt his feelings. It wasn't something that was easy to do. He had pretty thick skin. He probably shouldn't have come on this trip with her. He'd gotten it in his head that she'd see how he felt and reciprocate.

And he thought, after yesterday, they'd made progress in that area.

But now it was clear that she'd never have feelings for him, no matter how much he tried to tell himself to be patient.

If, after that kiss, she didn't want another one, it was over.

He would just have to settle for being her friend. He didn't like it, but he could live with it.

CHAPTER 21

*D*ani couldn't stand the thought that she'd hurt Grayson's feelings. She hadn't meant to. But she was still recovering from the first kiss and didn't think she could handle another one. Even with Jeremy around.

Grayson basically ignored her all the way through the horseback riding and the sugar plantation. He kept his arm around her and made it look like they were in love, but he always made sure they were with other couples, and a wall had come up between them. He barely said two words to her.

By the time they got onto the boat for the dinner cruise, Dani was ready to cry. They ate dinner with Jenny and Mike, and Grayson kept the conversation lively. During dinner, a band played, and as soon as dessert was over, Sonya and Steve took to the dance floor. The music was slow and romantic.

Someone tapped her on the shoulder. Jeremy stood there with his hand held out. "Can I have this dance?"

Dani wanted to say no. She should say no, but a part of her wanted Grayson to rescue her. To tell Jeremy that he was dancing with her instead. But he didn't say anything.

Fine. If he was going to be that way, two could play this game.

She slid her hand into Jeremy's. "Of course."

Jeremy led her onto the dance floor, and he held her close. He didn't say anything as they moved in a slow circle. He smelled like he always did, of a cologne that she bought him.

"I miss you," he said.

Dani didn't respond. Because she didn't miss him. Not really. She missed being in a relationship. She missed the future she thought she'd have. But she didn't miss him. Being with Grayson had opened her eyes up to a new possibility. Though, she'd have to find someone a little less good-looking. But there was no reason she couldn't find a nice guy.

"Come on, Dani, when are you going to wake up? Grayson isn't the guy for you. He's in a whole different class, and you'll never fit into his world. I know I'm not perfect, but I love you."

The song ended, and Dani let go of him. "Thank you for the dance."

Then she walked away and leaned on the edge of the boat, watching the sun dip lower and lower into the water. Jeremy was right, and she hated that reality. She'd never been good enough for Grayson. He was better than her in every way. Well, maybe not every way. He had ruined her day after all.

A figure moved up to her side, and Dani glanced over. Grayson stood there with two glasses of champagne and handed her one, still trying to make it look like they were in love for Jeremy's sake. She was tired of acting.

After a few moments, he spoke. "I'm sorry that Jeremy ruined your day."

She scoffed. "Jeremy? He didn't ruin my day."

"You've been quiet and sulky. I know you're not having fun."

"That has nothing to do with Jeremy." Grayson was so blind. She'd really thought he could read her better than that. "You, you idiot. It's you who ruined my day. I was perfectly fine, but you've been acting like I insulted your mother."

He scowled. "I have not."

"Have you uttered two words to me today? No.

You were fantastic at putting on a show for the others, but you basically ignored me. I don't even know what I did." Though, she really did, but she didn't want to admit that to him.

"Why did you dance with Jeremy? I thought you were getting over him." His voice came out harsh.

Tears pricked her eyes. "Because it would've been rude to say no. I waited for you to rescue me, but you didn't."

He put a hand on her shoulder. "I didn't think you needed rescuing. I was actually giving you a chance to stand up to him. I thought you might want that. In fact, I really thought you were going to throw your glass of wine in his face."

"Why would I do that?"

"Because he ruined your day."

She huffed. "How many times do I have to tell you. He didn't ruin my day. You did. Did you bother to ask me to dance? No. But he did. Maybe I should go back to him."

"You can't mean that." His face twisted, and he withdrew from her.

Except that maybe she did. "What future do I have to look forward to when I get home? Huh? A lonely apartment and an awkward job. If we make up, at least, things will be like they were before. We were comfortable before I pressured him into getting married."

She expected Grayson to respond to that, but he didn't. Instead, he took his glass of champagne and walked away, leaving her alone to watch the sunset. Dani kept her eyes firmly on the water, not wanting to see the couples all around her. She didn't want to envy them.

She should've known better than to go on this romantic day when there was no one to share in the romance. If she'd let him, Grayson would've pretended. He would've kissed her and made sure everyone else saw. But she didn't want fake. She wanted real.

But she wasn't allowed to have real. Real was for other people.

She wasn't worthy of anything real.

She couldn't help the tears that flowed down her cheeks, but luckily, there was no one there to see them.

CHAPTER 22

Grayson didn't know what Dani wanted. She was constantly hot and cold, and he hated this. She was his best friend, and now she was acting like a stranger. He knew that she was struggling with the emotional havoc Jeremy was heaping on her, but Grayson supposed he wasn't helping. His own damn feelings had gotten in the way.

Once they made it back to the cruise ship, she took off down a hall, and he let her go. They both needed some time to process what happened. He walked around the deck, listening to the waves and thinking. He hadn't wanted to push things with her because he didn't want to ruin their friendship, but it was halfway there already. More than halfway probably.

Things would never go back to normal for them, no matter how hard they tried. He never should've married her, and he certainly shouldn't have encouraged the idea of pretending to be a happily married couple. It made him want things he couldn't have. And now he'd never see her as anything other than his wife. He'd never be able to watch her in another relationship, and if she went back to Jeremy, there was no way he could stand by and watch that trainwreck.

At this point, he had nothing to lose by telling Dani how he felt. She'd tell him she felt the same way, or she'd tell him that she didn't like him like that.

Either way, he'd know for sure, and they'd be blissfully happy for the rest of their lives, or they'd have to find their way back to a new sort of friendship. But they had to get the elephant out of the room. He didn't know what he was waiting for.

He jogged back to the room and slipped inside. Dani sat on the balcony, her bronzed legs stretched out in front of her and her hair up in a messy bun. Her eyes were a little red, but he couldn't let that deter him from his mission, or he'd chicken out.

He opened the slider door and sat in the chair next to her.

"I've loved you for a long time," he said.

Dani was quiet for a moment. "I know. I love you too. You're my best friend."

Oh, this was going to be harder than he thought. But he couldn't let her derail him. He had to get this out. He swiveled in his seat so he was facing her. "No, you don't understand. I'm completely and totally in love with you, and I have been since we were freshmen in college."

She swallowed but wouldn't look at him. "Grayson, please don't do this. I can't lose you as my friend."

"And I'm not asking you to. Just hear me out, and if you don't feel the same way, I will find a way to shut the feelings off so we can still be friends. It might take a little bit, but I can do it. After the past few days, things feel weird anyway, so I might as well go all in."

"What do you mean?" she asked.

"I mean, I need you to know how I feel. I've been waiting for Jeremy to screw up bad enough that you told him to go to hell. I wasn't about to be a home-wrecker, and then your wedding happened. And now I see a future for us. I want to sign the wedding certificate. And when we get home, I want to find us a house and eventually have babies, and I want you by my side forever. I love you. Fiercely."

Her eyes glistened with tears, but she didn't say

anything. He had nothing more to add, so he waited, but she just stared at him, and then she looked away, off into the dark ocean. He knew it would take time for her to process what he just dumped on her, so he sat back in his chair and waited. It was extremely hard to not reach over and grab her hand though.

After a few moments, she stood. "I'm going to take a shower."

She slipped past without even looking at him. He let her go, not sure what to do now. He'd almost feel better if she'd told him that she didn't feel that way and to not ever bring it up again. But this silence was brutal. The unknown was a killer.

Though he supposed at this point, there was still hope. She didn't turn him down right away, so she might still take him up on his offer. He had to stay positive.

He went back inside and glanced at his watch. It was near midnight. He wasn't thinking clearly. He'd go to bed and then tell her he needed an answer of some kind in the morning so they could move forward. He owed her the night to think things over. This was a lot.

He collapsed into bed. He worried that he'd be awake for a while, worrying about things, but his eyes drifted shut quickly, and he was lost to dreamland.

CHAPTER 23

*D*ani stayed in the shower way longer than she normally would. It was easy to cry in there because then the tears were simply washed away. She wasn't sobbing, but the tears still flowed. This was what she worried about. Feared from the moment Grayson kissed her at her wedding and then even more so when she kissed him by the pool.

Grayson had ruined everything. He made it so that they could never be friends again. He'd just told her that he loved her. And as much as she wanted to love him back, she couldn't.

That was a lie. She could easily love him back, but deep down, she knew he could never really love her.

He might have thought he loved her, or maybe he was just lying, but Dani knew the truth. She was unworthy of a love like his, and he'd see that soon enough. She couldn't risk her heart by allowing him to love her because it would never last. She wasn't pretty enough or skinny enough or smart enough, and she wasn't sure how he didn't see that right now. He was blinded by their friendship and his need to rescue her.

If she gave in now, he might stick around for a few months, but then he'd see the real her and leave. Then she'd be even more heartbroken than she was now.

She'd always known she'd have to settle for a man like Jeremy. He wasn't awful, but he wasn't great either. He was the best she would be able to do long-term. Growing up, her father had belittled her and let her know exactly what kind of person she was.

And a boy in middle school had confirmed everything her father said when he'd told her he was just dating her because the pretty girls all turned him down. Then in high school, she finally found a guy she thought was incredible. He was sweet and cute, and before the end of the two months they dated, she handed him her v-card, and he dumped her the next day.

She found later that his best friend had bet him that it would take longer than three months for her to give it up.

That was who she was. The leftover girl.

Guys like Grayson didn't date the leftover girl unless they thought they had no other option.

So she had no idea what he was thinking. Because he had plenty of other options.

Unless he was just being noble, like those men she read about in regency novels. They were always sacrificing their own happiness to save the damsel in distress, but in the end, they fell in love with her anyway.

Grayson knew all this about her as well. She'd spilled her whole history for him one night their sophomore year in college when they'd both had a little too much to drink. That was right before she had to drop out.

But Dani wouldn't get her happily ever after. She'd end up divorced and without any friends.

She turned off the shower and dried off. That was it. She'd remind him why they could never be together and that she wanted to go back to just being friends.

He'd understand then. She just had to remind him of these things.

She quickly threw on a tank and shorts. She took a couple of deep breaths. She had to get ahold of herself and not cry.

She could do this.

She headed into the bedroom and spotted

Grayson on the bed. She climbed in next to him, ready to talk his ear off. It would be easy in the dark because then she wouldn't have to look him in the face.

But his breathing was deep and long.

He was fast asleep.

* * *

DANI DIDN'T SLEEP MUCH, and when she woke the next morning, Grayson was already gone. She reminded herself of all the things she had to tell him. Then she went downstairs and found him on the balcony with an array of breakfast food laid out before him. She was surprised to see him. She thought he might be in the gym, but also, she was kind of hoping she could put this off a little longer.

She plopped into the seat across from him, anxiety crawling in her stomach. "Hungry, are you?"

He grinned at her. "Starving, but you can have some if you want."

She was glad he wasn't acting all weird. That told her that if she explained everything now, they'd be fine. At least, she hoped so.

She nibbled on a piece of bacon and thought about how to begin.

"About last night…" she said.

He waved his hand. "Don't worry about it. You don't feel the same way, and I'll get over it. Our friendship can survive this."

She let out a breath. "It's not that...I just...well. You know I've told you about my dad and my dating history and everything. And, um, I just don't want you to see me the same way. I don't want to be your left-over girl. Or just the damsel in distress you're rescu-ing. Because that will never last."

He frowned and came around the table so he was sitting right next to her. "Are you saying that you don't want to date me because you don't think you're worthy of me?"

She swallowed. She knew he'd understand. "Yeah. I'm not, and I'd rather be your friend than an ex."

He laughed, and she felt stupid. She pushed at the arms of her chair to get up, but he moved into her space, so she couldn't.

"Dani," he said in a gentle voice. "Look at me."

She did, and his face was so serious. "I've known you for a long time. Don't you think that, if you really were the person you thought you were, I'd have seen it by now?"

Of course he did. He just wouldn't admit it to her. "Maybe. But I think you're just being noble. I'm not worth throwing your life away."

He gave her another infuriating grin. "Now that I

understand exactly why you're turning me down, I'm not taking no for an answer."

"What is that supposed to mean?"

"It means I love you, and with loads of compliments and reinforcements from me, someday maybe you'll love you too. And, Dani, you aren't my leftover girl. You're the one who got away and the one I've regretted letting go for all these years."

She barely had time to comprehend the words before his lips were on hers, and as much as she wanted to fight it, she couldn't. She melted into his arms, and for the first time in a long time, she felt like she was exactly where she belonged.

CHAPTER 24

*G*rayson didn't want to stop kissing Dani. For one thing, he was afraid she'd turn him down again. But also, he enjoyed it, and he wasn't ready for her to pull away. He'd woken up resigned to her rejection, and now that he knew how she really felt, he wasn't ready to let her go.

He held her close to him so she couldn't get away.

"Do you believe me, you beautiful girl?" It hurt him to think that she felt like a leftover girl who deserved so little.

She blushed. "No. But I guess it's too late now, so I'll just enjoy this while I can."

"You know, fifty years from now, you'll still be saying the same thing."

She chuckled. "Tell you what, once we hit our tenth anniversary, I'll stop thinking you're going to leave me."

It wasn't exactly what he wanted to hear, but he'd take it. Or maybe not. All of his dreams were falling into place, and he could finally share with her the things he'd been hoping for. "Is that negotiable? How about when you get pregnant with our first child?"

She twisted her lips back and forth, and Grayson resisted the urge to plant his on hers again. But he wanted to hear this answer.

"You really think that's gonna happen before we hit the ten-year mark?" She wouldn't look at him. He could see the wheels turning in her head.

They were definitely having kids before the ten-year mark. He'd have them right away if she wanted. "Do you remember before you started dating Jeremy, how we used to talk about our futures?"

"Yeah."

"Do you remember how many kids you said you wanted?"

She flushed. "Ten."

"What happened to that dream?"

She'd always loved kids and talked about her future children often. But shortly after she started dating Jeremy, she stopped.

"Ten was a ridiculous number. Nobody has that many kids anymore. Besides, Jeremy wanted me to help him open up another clinic. We'd be too busy, and he didn't really want any kids. I just figured we'd never have any."

Yet another reason to hate that bastard. He kept stealing her dreams. But Grayson had every intention of giving her everything she wanted.

"Well, if we're going to have ten, we need to get started."

Dani still wouldn't look him in the eye. "But you only wanted two."

"I've changed my mind. Ten is a good number." He'd never thought much about how many kids he wanted. He always said two because that's what people expected, he just figured that would be a decision he and his someday-wife would have. And his someday-wife now wanted ten kids, so ten it would be.

"Maybe not ten." She gave a nervous giggle.

He shifted a bit and pulled her into his lap. "Then how many?"

She fiddled with the buttons on his shirt. "Four?"

"Four sounds good. But I still don't think we should wait forever. In fact, I'm totally down with spending the day hiding in here and trying. We can have room service all day."

Her eyes widened, and she leapt off his lap. "It's our last sea day!" She ran back into the room and returned with the daily itinerary. Three-quarters of it was highlighted. He wondered if she was scared to sleep with him or just excited about the day.

Her eyes sparkled as she rattled off the list of things she wanted to do. "In twenty minutes, there's a yoga class. Then Harry Potter trivia—you and I will rock that. We can go to the art auction, and there's another wine tasting. Oh, and we can watch the belly flop contest, and then I'm dying to do the cooking class." She met his eyes and pouted. "I never get to do fun stuff like this at home, and I don't know when we'll be on another cruise, so I want to take advantage of it." She swallowed and looked at him again. "Then tonight we can start on baby-making. Is that okay? I hope you're not too disappointed. But I really want to do all this stuff, and I don't want to rush sex."

He leaned forward and pressed his lips against hers again. "We can wait as long as you want. I'm ready whenever you are, and it doesn't have to be tonight or even this week." He meant it too. He didn't want her to feel pressured into anything. He hoped things would happen faster rather than slower, but he was okay if they didn't.

She nodded and gave him a relieved smile. "Okay then. Let's go do yoga."

She jumped up and took his hand. He wasn't sure how the day would go, but at least, she was officially his. He didn't have to hold anything back anymore, and he could kiss those gorgeous lips whenever he wanted.

Grayson finally had everything.

CHAPTER 25

So far, this day had been the best Dani ever had in her life. She'd fantasized about being with Grayson in the past, of course, and wondered what that would be like. Those were moments in the middle of the night when she couldn't help her thoughts. But reality had far exceeded expectations.

Grayson kept his hands on her in some way at all times. Except during yoga, but that wasn't for lack of trying. The instructor told Grayson if he didn't stay on his own mat, he would kick him out of the class.

Her skin tingled every time his flesh met hers. And a part of her wondered if they shouldn't skip the rest of the activities and just hang out in their room. But she still worried about that. In spite of his insistence that she was beautiful and everything he ever wanted, sleeping together could change that. She could totally disappoint him.

So she kept him out on the boat. Doing all the things.

During Harry Potter trivia, he kept his arm around her and gave her a kiss every time she got a correct answer to a question. They won and now had a Harry Potter tote bag and lanyard.

"Why don't we head back to the room for lunch? Then we'll hit up the art auction," Grayson said.

Dani shook her head. "If we go to the room, we'll never leave."

He wrapped his arms around her and pulled her close. "Would that be so bad?" Then he kissed her long enough for her to consider it. But she pulled away. "Yes. Art auction. Belly flop contest. Cooking class. Dinner. Magic show."

His eyes sparkled, and he ground his hips into hers. "I'll show you magic."

She blushed and giggled. "I'm sure you will. But not until I do all the things I want to do." Maybe by then, they'd be so tired that he wouldn't notice how bad she was in bed.

"Okay. Let's go eat." She worried that maybe he was disappointed.

They managed to snag a seat overlooking the

water. Dani hit up the taco bar, and Grayson went for the pasta and salad.

"The water is so peaceful," Dani said.

"It is." They stayed quiet for a moment, and she appreciated the peace they had together. It was just so easy with him.

"So where do you want to live?" Grayson asked, watching her instead of the water.

Dani hadn't thought about that. Obviously, they couldn't live at her place, and his was a few hours away, and there was her job to consider. She knew he could live anywhere since most of the businesses he owned were basically run by other people. "With you," she said with a grin.

"I know that. But I didn't know if you wanted to stay in the same town. My house is kind of a bachelor pad. We could live anywhere really. We could live on a cruise ship if you wanted."

Dani's eyes widened. She'd never heard of that. It seemed so out there. "That's a thing?"

"It is."

Dani chewed on her bottom lip. "That's tempting." And it was. Constantly being waited upon by others. The sea every day. But it would never work.

Grayson chuckled. "I'll make a call."

The fact that he could so easily make that call made her a little uneasy. "No. Don't. I don't know that

I could be away from my mom like that. Also, where would I work?"

"Dani, you don't have to work anymore."

"I know, but I like my job." Which was mostly true. She did love animals. She didn't like working with Jeremy, but she'd manage.

"Okay, so no living aboard cruise ships. You could go back to school if you wanted, fulfill your dreams of becoming a veterinarian."

She gave a slow nod. Maybe. Or maybe he was just trying to make sure she was well educated so he didn't have to say he married a college dropout. Honestly, she wasn't sure she even wanted to become a vet anymore. She liked working with the animals, but there were other ways she could do that. She could volunteer at a shelter or work at a doggy daycare.

"And if I didn't want to go back to school? What if I just want to stay home with you and raise babies?"

"Then that's what we'll do. I just want to make sure you get what you want. Maybe we get a big house on the lake somewhere with a small cottage house for your mom. That way she can be close, but we don't have to stay in town."

"I actually like that idea a lot. But, Grayson, you're talking about a lot of money." Big houses on the lake were millions of dollars.

Grayson reached over and put a hand over hers. "We're married. What's mine is yours."

She took a sip of her soda. "Exactly how much are we talking?"

Grayson rubbed his nose. "A lot."

"Come on, Grayson, now is not the time to be shy about this." She and Grayson were incredibly open about a lot of things, but they usually didn't talk about money because it made her uncomfortable. However, if he was serious about sharing, then she wanted to know. They'd gone all-in on this, and she was feeling braver now with him than ever before, and she didn't know if it would last.

Grayson dug his phone out of his pocket and opened an app, showing it to her. "This is what's in my checking and savings." He pointed at the amount.

Dani's eyes widened. She'd never seen so many zeros before in a bank account.

He scrolled to the left. "And this is what's in my investment accounts."

Dani choked on her Coke. That was the kind of money that people only dreamed of. It could not be real.

"You okay?"

She coughed, and Grayson patted her back.

"I'm fine. You could probably pay cash for a house on the lake with a cottage house." She'd always known he had money, but she always thought it was just comfortable, not obscene.

"Yeah, so?" He didn't seem to understand why she was shocked. Maybe he thought most rich people had that kind of cash, but he was beyond rich.

"So. This is going to take some getting used to."

"Okay. Whatever you need."

"Just some time. Speaking of, what time is it?"

Grayson glanced at the phone. "We should get going if you want to be a part of the art auction. We can get a few pieces for our new house."

Dani nodded, still dumbstruck. She really didn't have to work anymore if she didn't want to.

And maybe she didn't. Maybe she'd volunteer at the local animal shelter a few times a week. Maybe there were more benefits than just being married to her best friend.

CHAPTER 26

"So I think it's time for you two to share your story," Sonya said. They only had two more days left on the cruise, and so far, she and Steve were still as handsy as ever. Though, at this point, Grayson couldn't blame them. He couldn't bear to be more than a few inches away from Dani, but that was mostly because he was afraid if he did, she'd change her mind.

Again.

But he didn't think she would. Once she let her guard down, she'd been the most relaxed and happy he'd ever seen her. It was a side of her he didn't see often, and it was his favorite. He'd hoped they'd end up back in their room, but instead, they were at dinner with all the other honeymooning couples.

"Oh, ours is a good one," Dani said. "We've been best friends for forever. But we never really dated. And in college, I was dating Jeremy."

"Wait. As in the Jeremy that was on our excursion?" Sonya asked, sipping her soda.

"The one and only," Dani said with a grimace.

"You're right. This is a good story. Continue."

"Anyway, Jeremy and I got engaged, and Grayson was my man of honor."

Grayson leaned forward, grabbing a roll from the bowl in the middle. "I feel like I need to interrupt here before she goes any further. I've been in love with her for a long time, but I didn't want to ruin her relationship. I was kinda hoping it would just work itself out. Keep that in mind as she finishes her story."

Every person at the table was riveted by Dani and Grayson's story. Grayson had to admit that it was a good one.

"Anyway, Jeremy left me at the altar, said he couldn't do it. Grayson stood in and took his place." She slid her hand on Grayson's knee and squeezed. Her ring flashed in the sunlight. The ring that Jeremy was supposed to give her, but Grayson did instead. "I've never been happier."

"So why is Jeremy on the boat?" Sonya asked.

"Because the idiot thought we could still go on a honeymoon even though he didn't marry me." She grinned to try to show that it didn't bother her, but it still stung when she thought about it.

Sonya cackled. "That's some nerve. You and Grayson are super cute together. Oh, guys, I have the best idea. We should do this again next year on our anniversary. All book the same cruise and make sure we end up as dinner buddies."

"I'm down with that," Dani said, and everyone else readily agreed. Grayson wasn't crazy about the idea, but the fact that Dani was thinking long-term was a good thing for them.

Dinner went quickly, and they left and took a walk around the deck. They stopped and stared out over the waves, the moon high in the sky. Grayson dropped a kiss on Dani's neck and trailed his lips up to her ear.

"Are you sure we have to go see the magic show?" he asked. She giggled and wiggled away from him.

"Yes. I want to see the magic show. I've never seen one."

"If you skip this one, I'll take you to Vegas in a couple of weeks, and we'll see the best ones. The one on the ship probably won't be very good. Come on, Dani, I'm beginning to think you're scared to go back to the room with me."

She dropped her eyes, and Grayson realized that she was. He was being an ass. He stepped forward and

drew her close to him. "I'm sorry. I'm pushing you.
Let's go see the magic show, and when we get back to
the room, we'll just make out. No sex until you're
ready."

She swallowed and shook her head. "It's not that.
It's just that…well…what if I disappoint you? I'm…
not very good."

Not very good? There was only one reason she
would feel like she wasn't good in bed.

When they got off the boat, he was totally
punching Jeremy in the nose. He'd done nothing but
make Dani feel like crap about herself and now this.
What man told a woman she's not good in bed? An
asshole. That's who.

"That can't possibly be true. Haven't we already
established that Jeremy is a douchecanoe who knows
nothing about women? I imagine that it's him who's
bad in bed, not you."

She still wouldn't look at him. "But what if I am?"

He dropped a kiss on her nose. "Look, I've been
with women before who've had similar concerns, and
usually it's just because other men have made them
feel bad about themselves when it wasn't true. But
you know what? If it doesn't go perfect the first time,
we'll work on it. Like really super hard. Like every
day." He gave her a cheeky grin. "Sometimes it takes
time to learn what your partner wants. And maybe

there's something you'll tell me that I need to work on too."

She swallowed. "Okay then. But you're taking me to Vegas next week."

Then she grabbed his hand and dragged him toward their room. This was a night he'd been looking forward to for a very long time, and he couldn't believe it was finally here.

He was about to show Dani a night she'd never forget.

CHAPTER 27

*D*ani blinked her eyes open. She wasn't sure what time it was, and quite frankly, she didn't care. She'd had a very long night, and she was planning on sleeping in until at least ten. She didn't care what she missed on the ship today. She flipped over and saw that Grayson was sound asleep.

She grinned. He'd been right. Last night was probably the best night of her entire life, and she'd get to repeat it every day from here to eternity. Today, she'd make Grayson pull out those marriage certificates, and they were signing them before he could change his mind.

Worthy of him or not, she wasn't letting him go.

Not after what he did to her last night. She shivered and thought about waking him up but didn't have the heart to. He deserved his rest.

She glanced at the clock. It was already after noon.

So much for getting up at ten.

She stretched and slipped out of bed. She took a quick shower and slid on a tank and some shorts. Grayson still hadn't stirred.

She scribbled a quick note telling him she was taking a walk and slipped out of the room, hoping she didn't wake him. He deserved his sleep, but today they were supposed to dock in the Bahamas, and she wanted to watch the boat pull in. It was on the opposite side of the ship from the one their room was on, so she had to stand on the deck.

She couldn't keep the grin off her face as she made her way up a flight of stairs and onto the deck. The boat was just pulling up, and she could hear people yelling instructions at one another below.

She wasn't sure how long she stood there, but she was fascinated by the guys tying up the boat and all the hustle and bustle down below. She didn't have any shore excursions booked, but Grayson said there was some decent shopping, and he wanted to see if they could find a ring. She had a ring on her finger, but it was the one Jeremy had given her. Grayson was just the one who slid it on. She didn't want this one anymore. She tugged on it and looked at it. It was probably just a fake diamond anyway. She let it drop into the water below.

Good riddance.

A hand slid around her waist, and she grinned.

"I was wondering how long it would take you to find me," she said and spun around to show Grayson her naked finger. But then her smile fell. "Jeremy," she said and swallowed.

His arm tugged her closer. All her happy feelings disappeared. This was a man who'd done nothing but show her misery, and here he was acting like he still owned her.

His face was pained as he stared at her. "I'm so sorry. I miss you. I've been an idiot."

She tried to step away but was trapped between him and the railing. "It's too late," she said feeling small. But she couldn't let him get to her. "Honestly, it was too late when you left me at the altar. Thank you for that. If you hadn't, I would've never known what true love looked like."

He squeezed his eyes shut. "I know. I just had so much baggage with weddings and marriage, and it all came crashing down at the wrong time. I'm sorry, Dani. Let me make it up to you."

She let out an ironic laugh. "It's too late for that."

He had no idea how late. She might've taken him back yesterday if he'd come to her with this sob story, but not today. Not ever.

She put her hands on his chest to push him away, but before she could, he closed the distance between them and pressed his lips against hers. At first, she was so shocked that she didn't react.

Then she shoved him hard. "Get off of me. I told you that I'm with Grayson now. We're married, and that's never going to change. You're too late."

She turned and stormed away, but he grabbed her hand. "Dani, please."

She walked into an open doorway and shook him off. "If you touch me one more time, I'll find a security guard and tell him that you are harassing me."

He rolled his eyes. "Fine. Whatever. But don't come crawling back when he dumps your fat ass. This was your last chance."

He walked away, and she clenched her fists, trying not to cry. She didn't know why she cared what he thought anymore, but she did. His words stung. She took a couple of deep breaths. Grayson never talked to her that way. In fact, he'd never once made her cry. Okay, maybe once, but that was because she was being an idiot.

She was right under the buffet. She'd grab a couple

of plates of his favorites and take them back to the room, and they'd have lunch in there and maybe spend the rest of the day in bed.

She could see the Bahamas another day.

CHAPTER 28

Grayson didn't expect to wake up alone. He hoped Dani hadn't run off on him again. He fumbled for his phone and saw that it was twelve-thirty. No wonder she left. He was cramping her style of doing all the things she'd wanted. He grinned. One of the things he loved about her was her zeal for life. She'd never really given him the chance to spoil her before, and now he planned on going all-in. He couldn't wait to start their life together. Buy her dream house and have a family.

He stretched and sat up, flicking on a light. Next to him was a note. He read it over quickly. It said she was going for a walk but didn't say what time she'd be back or when she left. He hopped into the shower and figured if she wasn't back by the time he got out, he'd go looking for her.

Thirty minutes later, he was dressed and ready to go, but Dani was nowhere in sight. He left the room, walked over to the other side of the boat, and glanced down. They'd just docked. He wondered if she watched it. This was not a good floor for it though. He jogged down three flights of stairs and found lots of people watching the boat get tied up. He looked around for her but didn't see her. This was impossible. He'd never find her. He should probably head back to the room and just wait for her. She wouldn't leave him alone all day. Not after the night they had. At least, he hoped not. He was about to head back when he saw a flash of her hair up in a bun.

For a second, he couldn't tell what he was looking at. But then reality crashed down. She was there with Jeremy. *Kissing* him.

Grayson stood frozen to the spot. He was far enough away that he couldn't hear their conversation but close enough that he could see everything. After the kiss, Jeremy took her hand, and they went back inside the boat.

Anger coursed through his veins, but he knew better than to chase after her. He'd just say something he regretted. Plus, he didn't want to walk in on any more kissing scenes.

In all his wildest imaginations, this was the last thing he expected to see. The thought that she'd go running back to Jeremy was so far down the realm of possibilities that he could barely even fathom it.

His heart was broken, but his anger overrode that. After last night, she jumped right back into Jeremy's arms. It seemed so strange to him that she could do something like that. It completely went against her entire personality.

He'd never known her to be someone who could be callous and cold. But he couldn't deny what he saw. It wasn't like it was a misunderstanding. They were kissing, and they walked off hand in hand.

How could Grayson be so misled by the whole thing? By her?

He continued walking around the boat, trying to figure out what to say to Dani. He loved her too much to yell at her, but he wouldn't just let this go either. He had to tell her how much she hurt him. He had to know why she'd do something like this.

"Yoohoo, Grayson, is that you?"

Grayson turned around. Sonya and Steve were right behind him. "What are you doing without your lovebug?" Sonya asked, leaning into Steve.

"Just taking a walk." His fist clenched unconsciously. "I'm not sure where she is. She was gone when I woke up. Probably wanted to see the boat dock."

He tried to keep the hurt out of his voice. He didn't need everyone else to know his business.

"Oh, well, in that case, we're heading up to lunch. Do you want to join us?"

He almost turned them down, but then his stomach growled. He hadn't eaten yet today, and he'd probably think clearer on a full stomach. Maybe then he could talk to Dani without yelling.

Or crying.

It was a fifty-fifty possibility at this point.

And to be honest, he didn't know the last time he cried. Probably when his sister died.

"Sure, I'll come to lunch with you." It would help to be with other people while he thought this through. They'd distract him.

They wove their way through the crowds of people and up a few stairs. Grayson was still trying to work out how Dani could do such a thing. All he could see was her and Jeremy kissing. He'd seen it before, of course, but this time, it dug right into him.

Maybe lunch with Sonya and Steve was a bad thing. He might spill his guts to them.

"Hey, guys," he said. "I think I'm just gonna grab a couple of plates and head back to our room and see if Dani is there." He might as well keep up the charade.

This way he could eat and clear his head and not worry about anyone else.

"Oh, isn't that cute? You've only been away from each other for a few minutes, and already you miss her." Sonya planted a kiss on Steve. "Though I totally understand. Steve and I haven't been out of each other's sight since we got on the boat. I'm really not looking forward to going home to real life."

Home.

Real life.

Without Dani.

He'd pictured their life together and allowed himself to fantasize about what came next. He was ready for the next step.

He'd really thought they'd be signing those marriage certificates and living happily ever after.

But he was wrong.

CHAPTER 29

*D*ani waited in line for the stir fry. It was a surprisingly long line, and she worried that she'd been gone a little too long from Grayson. He was probably awake by now and looking for her. She should've gone straight back there after she watched the boat dock.

Well, after Jeremy accosted her. She couldn't believe his nerve, and she wondered what she ever saw in him. She'd have to bring Grayson with her when she went to the house to get her stuff because who knew what Jeremy would try. His sheer obliviousness to everything was shocking. She might even have to file a restraining order. Grayson would help her with that if she needed it.

"Hey, Dani," a voice said, and Dani spun around.

Jenny and Mike were right behind her. They were hand in hand, much more tan than the first day she'd met them. Though that sure beat the lobster-red of Sonya and Steve. She nearly giggled at the thought. It hadn't kept them from still pawing each other every chance they got.

"Oh, hey."

A woman walked by with a cart of desserts, and Dani eyed them. She'd have to grab a cheesecake and a few cookies before she went back to the room as well. She wasn't sure when they'd emerge again.

"You going shopping today?" Jenny asked, bouncing on her toes.

"Yeah, Grayson said there were a lot of great jewelry shops on the island." She couldn't wait to get back to him but wasn't sure if she would tell him about Jeremy or not. She didn't want Grayson to do something stupid and get in a fight, so maybe she'd just wait until they got off the boat.

But then he might think she was keeping things from him.

Oh, this was impossible. Why did Jeremy have to put her in this situation? That man was still ruining her life even after he was no longer a part of it.

"There she is!" a voice shouted, and Dani looked up. Heading for them were Sonya and Steve. Right behind them was Grayson. Her heart swelled at the sight of him.

They could eat the food here before it got cold. Then they'd either head out onto the island or go back to the room. Dani actually didn't care which one. As long as she got to spend the day with him.

Dani grinned at him, but he didn't smile back. In fact, he looked a little angry. Maybe he was upset that she left him. Or maybe he wasn't angry about her at all. Maybe something happened on the way to the buffet. She had to stop being so paranoid. Grayson loved her. He wasn't Jeremy, but it would probably take some time before she stopped worrying that he was going to do something mean.

She stepped out of the line and approached him, grabbing his hand. He shook her off. "Don't you dare touch me," he said in a voice louder than he normally spoke.

Dani recoiled, her stomach twisting. "I'm sorry I left. I just wanted to see the boat dock." She'd never seen Grayson behave like this. Maybe he was different in a relationship than he had been in a friendship.

"That's not what I'm talking about. I didn't think you were the type of girl who went straight from one man's bed to another. But I guess I was wrong." He was speaking way too loud. Everyone was listening.

"What are you talking about?"

He shoved his hands into his air and gritted his teeth. "I saw you with Jeremy."

Dani let out a breath of relief. That was something she could fix, but not here in front of all those people.

"Listen, that was not what it looked like. I can explain, but let's go back to the room."

Grayson scoffed. "Explain? It was pretty obvious what was going on there. There's no way to explain. We're done. Don't bother talking to me again."

He stormed away, and Dani looked around. All their new friends were staring at them. She swallowed, her hands shaking. Jenny stepped forward. "Are you okay?"

She shook her head. She didn't know if she'd ever be okay. How could Grayson just dismiss her like that? He didn't know the whole story, and Dani wasn't sure if he ever would. He told her to never speak to him again, and she was scared that he meant it.

Did she really just lose the one person in her life that she couldn't live without? All because her asshole ex-fiancé tried to get back together with her. And she didn't even want him.

Her eyes pricked, and she knew the tears were coming. She didn't want to lose it right there in front of all their friends. Not only had Grayson yelled at her, but he'd also embarrassed her. Even Jeremy didn't do things like that.

She turned and ran for the nearest bathroom outside of the buffet. She found the farthest stall, raced into it, and threw the lock.

Then she let out a quiet sob and sank to the floor.

CHAPTER 30

G rayson had no idea what to do now. He'd lost it on Dani and hadn't meant to. Well, he meant that he never wanted to talk to her again, but he hadn't meant to be so rude about it or do it in front of so many people. But she'd caught him at a bad time when he was still freshly hurt.

He headed for the casino and sat down at a Texas hold 'em table. Gambling wasn't a habit of his, but it was something that would pass the time. He handed the dealer a few hundred and ordered a gin and tonic.

He lost his first hand, but only because he wasn't paying close enough attention. How could he after what happened to him? Maybe the casino was a bad idea. Then again, maybe it was just what he needed.

He didn't care how much money he lost. This was about drinking and gambling away his pain.

A few more people joined the table, and Grayson finished his drink and ordered another. He managed to win a few hands and lose even more. He didn't care about the money. At this point, he'd lost the one thing that mattered the most to him in the entire world.

Dani.

He didn't know if he could live without her.

Several hours later, eight thousand bucks down, and after countless gin and tonics, he left the casino. He wasn't sure if Dani returned to the room or not, but he wasn't about to sleep out on the deck. She was the one who left him, not the other way around.

She'd probably already grabbed her stuff from the room and moved it in with Jeremy. She'd sleep with him. Grayson gritted his teeth. He didn't want to think about her with that bastard. Grayson should've punched him when he had the chance.

Maybe he still would.

He had trouble getting his keycard in but eventually got the door to swing open. The room was dark, and the curtains still firmly closed from this morning. Grayson was unsteady on his feet as he crossed the floor. He didn't think they'd undocked yet, but maybe the boat was moving.

Or maybe he was just really drunk.

It was hard to say which one.

And it didn't really matter.

He managed to cross the room and open the curtains. The night sky winked down at him. The sea was calm. They were still in port, so he was definitely drunk. He couldn't remember the last time this had happened. He usually only had a drink or two when he went out. He didn't like feeling out of control. Hopefully, Dani didn't come back tonight, or he might do something stupid like beg her to stay with him.

Which is exactly what he wanted to do, but there was no way he would be the other man. She'd made her choice, and it wasn't him. That hurt, but the pain was dulled by his current state. Tomorrow morning, he wouldn't feel so good. But that would be better than the heartache of earlier.

He stumbled up the stairs and into the bathroom. He washed his face and brushed his teeth and then went to the bedroom.

He half-expected to see Dani in bed since it was already dark, but she wasn't there. In her place were rose petals and fancy towel critters. A bottle of champagne sat on the end table.

Had Grayson ordered that? He couldn't remember.

But he wasn't about to spend a night on a rose-petal-strewn bed alone.

He turned and stumbled down the stairs. It took him a few tries, but eventually, he managed to wrench the glass slider open. He sank onto a chair and watched the waves.

His head pounded, and the thoughts he'd been trying so hard to avoid came unbidden to his mind.

Dani had betrayed him in the worst way. He might've been okay if this happened earlier in the week. He'd still be sad, but they'd at least be friends. At this point, he wasn't sure if he'd ever be able to even look at her face again.

After what was the best night of his life, she'd gone and walked back into Jeremy's arms.

How could she?

Then to act like she'd done nothing wrong.

That wasn't Dani's style at all. Grayson didn't know what had gotten into her, but she'd changed.

Maybe he'd move out of Michigan. Find a change of scenery and forget all about Dani. He'd always wanted to try renting an apartment in Italy, but he'd never been willing to leave her behind.

In the morning, he'd call his assistant and see if she could find him a place in Tuscany. She'd be upset with him for bailing on her without warning for a week, but really, she ran his company better than he did. He was more of a figurehead at this point.

He laid his head back and closed his eyes.
He couldn't wait to get off this ship.

CHAPTER 31

*D*ani spent most of the day hiding out in the bathroom or places on the ship no one went to, like the library. She ventured back into the room briefly and grabbed a change of clothes and her bathing suit.

She had no idea where she would stay tonight, but certainly not with Grayson after he said all those mean things to her. As far as she was concerned, they'd probably never speak again. She couldn't believe he wouldn't even hear her out.

But now she was on a cruise ship without a room.

As darkness fell, Dani scoped out the lounge chairs on the deck that she could sleep on. A few were the round chairs with sunshades. She'd seen people sleeping on them earlier in the week. No one would even notice. Thankfully the trip was almost over.

"Dani." She spun around. Jeremy stood there, drink in hand.

Her heart fell. She'd hoped for a moment that the voice was Grayson, but of course, it wasn't. She'd fall right back into his arms if he asked her to.

"Get the hell away from me," she said and threw her stuff onto the chair. As much as she was angry with Grayson, Jeremy was completely a no-go. She was past him now.

He smiled sheepishly at her. "Come on, Dani. I know we've had a rough go of it this week, but do you think it's possible to still be friends?"

She braced herself, unsure how to answer that. Her feelings were all mixed up. She didn't love him anymore, but for some reason, she couldn't just tell him to go away. She should. She knew she should.

"I don't know." She should've said no. She knew that by giving him an opening, he'd run with it. But she desperately did not want to be alone.

Jeremy took a step closer. "Where's Grayson?"

She shrugged. "I don't know. He saw you kiss me and got mad."

Jeremy sniffed. "Well, now he knows how I feel."

Why was she even listening to him? "It's not the same thing. You left me for no good reason."

"For the last time, I didn't leave you. I just didn't want to get married."

She wondered if he'd ever realize how wrong that was. She leaned on the railing and looked out over the sea. "I fail to see the difference."

Jeremy glanced at the things on the chair. "Were you planning on sleeping there?"

Dani eyed him. "Maybe."

"Don't be stupid. You can stay with me." He nudged her.

She shook her head. "I'm done with you. Even if Grayson stays mad at me, we're not getting back together."

"I know that. You made that very clear earlier. But you can't sleep out here. I'll have the guy that cleans the room separate the beds. It will be fine. It's just a place to sleep. Not to sleep together."

This was why she had loved Jeremy. He may not have been the best person in a relationship, but he always looked out for her when she needed it. Sure, he said things that made her feel bad sometimes, but all men did that. Well, all the men in her life anyway.

"You know, that sounds really nice. Thank you."

It took a bit to find the guy who could separate the beds, and when they finally got into the room—a tiny interior one—Dani was beyond exhausted.

She changed in the claustrophobic bathroom and

then collapsed onto the bed. Dani didn't want to talk. She just wanted to sleep. But as soon as the lights were out, Jeremy couldn't seem to keep his mouth shut.

"You know I told you this would happen," he said. His voice was low and soft, but she knew he meant for her to hear.

"What?" she asked, feeling trapped now in this tiny, dark room. Jeremy's words could hurt her, and she'd walked right back into a situation where he could do it again.

"Guys like Grayson don't stay with women like you."

Dani swallowed.

"What's that supposed to mean?"

"Oh, come on. You have to know. I mean, you're uneducated and overweight. Kinda plain." Then he chuckled. "I bet I know what happened. You slept with him, didn't you?"

Dani twisted the sheets in her fists. Everything he said was true. But she hated that he'd managed to find her weak points early on in their relationship and stick a knife right into them. That's why he was an ass.

"You know, if I'm really that bad, why do you stay with me?" she asked. She needed to stand up to him and be done with him once and for all. She should've never put herself in this situation again, but here she was.

He sniffed. "Well, if I looked like Grayson and had his kind of money, I wouldn't. I could if I wanted to. But I felt sorry for you. You need somebody strong in your life."

He didn't say anything more, and soon she heard his soft snores.

His words played over and over in her head like a broken record. *"You slept with him, didn't you?"*

Maybe Grayson was looking for an excuse. Jeremy gave voice to every fear she already had, which meant they weren't just in her head. They were reality. She hated it and hated that she'd lost Grayson. He'd been her everything, and now he was nothing.

Now Dani had a choice to make, and she wasn't sure what the decision would be. Grayson was out of the question, but did she want to make a go of it with Jeremy or not?

CHAPTER 32

*G*rayson woke with a start. He blinked his eyes open at the blinding sun. Everything hurt. His entire body was a bright shade of red. Oh, this was not going to be a fun day.

Not only did his head hurt from the gin and tonics, but now he was completely sunburned. He staggered to his feet and hissed when he knocked his shins into the side table. He managed to make it inside and shut the sliding door.

He stumbled up the stairs, trying to ignore the pain. But every move was excruciating. He glanced in the mirror and groaned. He'd turned into a lobster.

Dani would laugh so hard.

Then his stomach clenched. Actually, she wouldn't because she wouldn't be talking to him ever again.

Man.

He'd screwed up.

And he didn't even know what he'd done to send her into Jeremy's arms. This was so absurd. He wanted her back. He needed to find her and beg her to reconsider.

But at the moment, he couldn't think straight. So, he picked up the phone and ordered coffee and a full breakfast. It was late. He probably could've ordered lunch, but he liked breakfast food. Then he found some ibuprofen and turned on the bath, making sure the water was cool.

His breakfast arrived just as he was getting out of the tub. He answered the door in a towel, and the woman bringing his breakfast eyed him. He thought she was checking him out, but she looked more concerned than anything.

"Would you like me to book you a treatment at our spa? They can help with sunburns."

"That's okay. I'll be fine. Thanks for offering." Though as soon as the words were out of his mouth, he regretted it. Maybe he should consider it. He hated being in pain.

He wanted to go back outside and eat but didn't want to risk more sun. He set up his breakfast at the table in the dining room and tried not to think about Dani.

But she was all he could think about.

He remembered clearly the night they met. She was stunning even then, but she never believed him when he told her.

He remembered the night he planned to kiss her for real instead of just two drunk kids. It was the Christmas party at his frat house his freshman year, and he had it all planned out. He even had mistletoe set up in the exact place he wanted to do it. They'd been friends the whole semester, but she seemed immune to all his hints that he wanted to be more than friends.

Then she hadn't shown up to the party.

He tried texting and calling with no response. That was not like her at all. She always responded immediately to him. It was one of the reasons he thought she felt the same way about him. They'd hit it off so fast.

Halfway through the party, he went down to her dorm and found her on her bed, crying her eyes out.

"My dad died," she said. Grayson knew she didn't have a great relationship with him, but sometimes those deaths were the worst because you didn't have time to fix them. The man was cruel and verbally abusive, but he was still her dad.

Grayson didn't remember what else happened that night, but he held her all night, even while they slept, and the next morning, she was gone. He'd kept up with her all the way through the funeral with texts and calls, reassuring her he'd be there for her the next semester.

Then two days before the new semester started, she called up again in tears. She had to stay home and help her mom. There was no coming back to school.

But it didn't change their relationship.

They talked every day, and during spring break, he went to visit her. It was the first time he met Jeremy, and Dani had introduced him as her boyfriend. He'd been crushed because she hadn't mentioned a boyfriend before, but Grayson wasn't about to give up that easily. He'd known from the beginning that she was his soul mate.

That summer, Grayson rented a beach house four doors down from Dani, and though they spent nearly every evening together—except Fridays—just hanging on the beach or doing something silly, Jeremy remained her boyfriend. She'd crushed his heart more times than he could count.

After that, he resigned himself to just being her friend.

Until this week.

Maybe that's what hurt the most. Before, he deluded himself into thinking that there was always a chance because she'd never outrightly rejected him.

And now she had.

Except she hadn't.

When he confronted her, she acted like there was an explanation. And maybe there was. Maybe he'd been stupid to assume that it was exactly what it looked like.

Maybe it wasn't what it looked like.

Though he wasn't sure how she would explain it away. The kiss was real enough.

Maybe his stupid pride was about to ruin the one relationship he'd always wanted. Over thirty seconds. He was ruining everything and being a baby about it. He had to find her and get the truth. He at least owed her that.

He jumped up but then realized he was still wearing just a towel. He raced upstairs and grabbed a t-shirt and a pair of basketball shorts. He had his wife to find.

He had to hear her out.

And if she was not planning on going back to the bastard, Grayson would kiss her senseless and never let her go again.

CHAPTER 33

*D*ani slipped out of the room before Jeremy got up. It was after ten, but it'd been late when they got back to the room. She hadn't slept well, her mind racing through all the possibilities of her future. None of which were something she wanted. She was certain she wouldn't get back together with Jeremy. He'd once again proven how cruel he was. But she was also just as certain that she wouldn't run back into Grayson's arms either. He'd shown her that she really wasn't worthy of his love.

She wandered up to the pool deck and sank onto one of the chairs. The cruise would be over tomorrow, and then she didn't have to worry about where she would sleep. Sure, she had to move out of her house, but her mom had a room she could stay in.

She'd do a lounge chair tonight. It wouldn't hurt her at all.

"Dani?"

Sonya stood there, all alone for the first time the entire trip. Dani almost didn't recognize her.

"Where's your other half?" Dani asked.

"Ah, he had a little too much to drink and is sleeping it off. Can I sit?"

Dani nodded even though she wanted to shake her head. Sonya had witnessed the scene the night before, and Dani didn't want to talk about it. Especially not with a woman she just met.

But to her surprise, Sonya didn't bring it up at all.

She just chattered on about her life at home and how it would change now that Steve was a part of it. Dani half-listened, her mind still on the things Jeremy said last night.

"I need help," Dani blurted, interrupting Sonya's story about her mom getting a new hot tub. Dani had no idea what persuaded her to ask for this, but she had nothing to lose.

Sonya stopped and just stared at her. "Of course. What's the matter?"

And before Dani could stop herself, she spilled the whole story to Sonya. From the moment Jeremy left her at the altar to the kiss she didn't want. She even told her all about the conversation she and Jeremy had the night before.

"And I don't know what to do," she finally said. "I love Grayson, but he's never going to talk to me again. Maybe Jeremy is right. But I don't want to be with him any longer either."

Sonya blinked at her, and Dani wondered if maybe Sonya was slower than she thought and couldn't process the story.

"What?" Dani asked.

"You know, I thought you were a smart one, and you probably are, but, girl, Jeremy is an asshole of the highest order. Though Grayson might be up there for the things he said yesterday. Maybe you just have bad taste in men."

She chuckled, but Dani didn't find it all that amusing. Sonya hopped off of her lounge chair and moved over to the edge of Dani's. Something about her demeanor changed as well.

"I have a Ph.D. in biomedical sciences." Her voice was different than normal. "I grew up very poor, but I was good at math and had teachers who saw great potential in me. I managed to get full scholarships all through my Ph.D."

"But you're working at IHOP," Dani said, completely dumbfounded by what Sonya just told her. Sonya sometimes acted like she was incredibly uneducated.

She smiled. "I am. Shortly after I graduated, I ended up working for a company that was doing some shady things. I was in the middle of it all, and after the endless lawsuits and interrogations, I left the field and took a job where no one would ever think to sue me. I actually managed to counter sue for some of the things that happened to me, and so I don't have to work, but I like having something to do, and waitressing keeps me in front of people. Education means nothing. Your worth comes from inside, and you are a sweet, caring, beautiful woman. You deserve better than Jeremy. Better than Grayson."

Dani choked up. No one but Grayson had ever told her those things before, and she didn't know what to say.

"But I want Grayson," she finally said. This was the truth.

Sonya grinned. "Well, then you're going to have to use your womanly wiles to convince him to at least hear you out. You owe yourself that. You're both stuck on this boat. Find him and tell him how you feel."

Dani nodded. She'd regret it if she didn't. Sonya was wiser than any of them. This woman had taken her completely by surprise.

"But I want you to promise me one thing." Sonya leaned forward, her face serious.

"What's that?"

"If you and Grayson don't get it all worked out, I want you to come find me. I'm in room 8521. Promise me that you will not spend the night with Jeremy again or sleep out on the deck."

Dani swallowed and nodded even though she would do no such thing. She wasn't spending the night in a room with the most affectionate honeymooners ever.

"Okay. I promise."

Sonya eyed her. "One more thing."

"What's that?"

"Please don't tell the others about my Ph.D. I like flying under the radar. No one ever expects anything of me, and I want to keep it that way. If people find out, they'll try to talk about high-level things, and I don't want Steve to feel left out."

"Does he know?"

"Of course. But he's still a little intimidated."

Dani understood that. Sometimes she felt that way with Jeremy because he had a degree, and she didn't.

Dani nodded.

Now she just had to find Grayson.

CHAPTER 34

*G*rayson looked everywhere for Dani, but she didn't seem to be on the damn boat. He even went as far as knocking on Jeremy's door, but no one answered. He wasn't sure what he would've done if he'd found her in there, but he really did have to talk to her. He wanted to convince her to stay with him.

He wandered aimlessly for a while, keeping an eye for her signature hair up in a knot. But she was nowhere. He supposed she could be moving around, and their paths hadn't crossed, but he was frustrated.

He found himself alone in the lounge with a bartender setting up. It was still fairly early, so he ordered a coffee instead of a drink. He wanted to be fully in control of himself when he finally found her. Alcohol would not fix that. He just hoped she hadn't really jumped right back into Jeremy's bed.

As he sat there, several people came and ordered drinks. Some crew started setting up in the front of the room. Probably trivia. He and Dani had gone to a couple and enjoyed them.

Maybe she'd come to this one. Perhaps she was still trying to do all the things on the ship. He'd wait and see if she showed up, and if she didn't, he'd go hunt down another event. He should've been doing that already. This was their last day, and she wouldn't want to miss it.

He watched as more and more people came, mostly couples. Steve and Michael chatted across the room. Maybe one of them had seen Dani. Steve had witnessed their argument, but it didn't matter. He didn't care what anyone thought anymore. Except for Dani.

"Hey, guys," Grayson said.

Steve gave him a grin. "I feel like we haven't seen you in forever, buddy."

"Yeah, you know. Dani and I wanted some alone time."

"And some fight time," Steve said with a chuckle, clapping him on the back. "You two make up?"

Grayson shook his head. "I was actually wondering if you guys had seen her. I have some apologizing to do."

"Oh yeah, she's up with our girls. They'll be here in a few minutes. They made us come early to get our names down."

"Names for what?" Grayson asked.

But before Steve could answer, he saw Dani. She'd just entered the room and looked around cautiously, but she didn't catch his eye. Sonya whispered something in her ear, and she laughed. Grayson loved seeing that smile. Normally, it was him that made her smile.

Steve smacked him. "Dude, are you even paying attention? We're hoping one of us gets picked."

"Sorry. The girls just got here," he said, pointing to the door. But they'd disappeared.

Michael gathered a few chairs around, enough for their whole crew, and dropped into one. Now that Grayson knew she was here, he decided to just wait. She'd come to him. Then he'd see if she'd leave so they could talk.

Sonya squealed when the girls approached. "This is so exciting. One of us is going to win the newlywed game."

Grayson groaned. Not another couple thing. He

glanced over at Dani, who stared at him, trepidation in her eyes. He was the one who told her to stay away, so he waved her over to him.

She dropped into the chair next to him. "I thought you never wanted to talk to me again," she muttered.

"I'm sorry. I was angry, and I overreacted. Please forgive me."

She let out a breath of relief. "Of course."

One hurdle out of the way. Forgiveness was one thing, but he wasn't sure if she was going to get back together with Jeremy.

"That doesn't mean you're off the hook. You still have some serious explaining to do."

She nodded. "I know. And this is not the place. But I want you to know that there is nothing between me and Jeremy. He's an asshole, and I didn't kiss him. He kissed me."

"We should maybe get out of here and talk about this."

But before they could, the cruise director got up and started speaking. Plus, Dani made no movement to leave.

"Welcome to the newlywed game. We will have three lucky couples come up and compete. The winner will get a bottle of champagne and dinner at one of our premium restaurants."

Grayson leaned over and whispered in her ear. "If you leave with me right now, I'll make sure you get both of those." He didn't really like these things, and he wanted to clear the air with her and make sure he understood where they stood.

She grinned. "When's the next time we get to watch a newlywed game? It's the experience, not the prize."

Grayson shook his head but settled back into his chair. At least, he knew they'd be okay now. Well, hoped so. He wasn't entirely sure what would happen after this. He and Dani had never fought before.

"Our first couple has been married twenty-two years. Folks, they'll be hard to beat. Welcome, Cindy and John."

A cheer went up, and a woman shot to her feet and clapped wildly. Her husband took her hand, and they about bounced to the front, huge smiles on their faces. They looked as happy as the honeymooners. Grayson hoped he and Dani were that way at twenty-two years. They just had to make it off this boat.

The next couple was announced—married ten years.

"And, of course, on the cruise we always have honeymooners. They never win, but they always try. Let's give a big cheer for Dani and Grayson."

Grayson groaned, but Dani jumped up and clapped her hands.

"We're going to cream them." She grabbed his hand, dragging him to the front of the room.

CHAPTER 35

*D*ani sat on the stage with Grayson, her hands shaking a little bit. She had no idea how this would go down. But honestly, this was better than going back to the room. She wanted to make up with Grayson, but she was still worried he would bail on her.

He was angry after all.

But at least he was holding her hand.

They all sat in the chairs, but before they got comfortable, the game show host had the girls up and out of the room.

Dani danced back and forth on her feet, not talking to the other two ladies. She should be more friendly, but in addition to wanting to win the game, she was nervous about what would happen afterward.

After several minutes, they were called back in.

"This is how the game works. We asked your husbands four questions. If you give the same answer they did, you get five points."

Dani sat down next to Grayson. They'd been friends for so long. This would be easy.

"First question. Where did you go on your first date?"

That was a hard one. Would Grayson have gone for the wedding or when they first hung out in college? She eyed him, but he didn't give any indication of what he said. The other couples answered first, and they both got it right. She could not embarrass herself.

The host shoved the mic in her face.

"The rooftop of the dorm building," she said hesitantly.

"Are you sure?" the host asked with a chuckle.

Dani swallowed and nodded.

"I thought for sure you'd get this wrong. No woman thinks the rooftop is an actual date, but that's what he said."

Grayson gave her hand a squeeze, and they moved on to the next question.

"What's the strangest place you and your spouse ever made whoopie?"

Oh crap. They'd only had sex once.

The first couple got two different answers—her boss's office and a McDonald's bathroom. Both of those sounded awful to Dani. The second couple got it right—the woods. Dani wondered how Grayson answered this. She went straight for honesty because that was the only way they'd get it right.

"A boat," she said, and everyone cheered.

The host winked at her. "What's your bra size?"

Grayson had been at all of her dress fittings, and so he knew her measurements by heart. Dani held her breath as the other couples answered, but they both got it wrong. She responded, and Grayson grinned before saying his matching answer.

They were the only ones who hadn't missed a question yet.

"What animal would your husband say best describes you?"

Oh no. Dani didn't want to get this question wrong. But she didn't have a clue.

Then a conversation they'd had a few years ago popped into her head. Grayson had told Dani that she was like a duck because she just let everything roll right off of her. It made no sense to her, so Grayson had to explain that duck's feathers don't absorb water, and it all rolls right off. He said it was something he really admired about her.

The first couple got it wrong. The second got it

right. To win, she had to give the correct answer. The host shoved the mic in her face again.

"A duck," she said.

Their little corner of newlyweds erupted into cheers. Grayson whooped, pulled her out of her chair, and kissed her full on the lips.

Maybe they wouldn't have such a hard time making up after all.

CHAPTER 36

*G*rayson was nervous as they went back to the room, champagne bottle in hand. This was their first big fight, and he wasn't sure what was coming next. Yes, Dani had said that she wasn't getting back together with Jeremy, but she hadn't said she wanted to stay with him either.

In fact, aside from the kiss at the end of the newlywed game, she'd barely touched him. Maybe she just wanted to be friends. Grayson didn't know if he'd be able to handle that.

They hung out with the other honeymooners for a bit after the game, but Grayson was itching to get back to the room and discuss things with Dani. He had to know where they stood.

He popped the door open, and Dani went in. She headed straight for the balcony.

"Uh, can we talk in here?" Grayson asked.

She turned, confusion on her face. The balcony was one of her favorite places on the boat. "Sure, but why?"

"Do you not see my face? I fell asleep on the balcony last night and didn't wake up until noon. My whole body is burned."

She let out a giggle. "It's not funny, I know it's not, but it kinda is." She reached for him but then dropped her hand.

"Whatever, I just don't want to go out there right now."

"Sure. No problem. Why did you sleep out on the balcony?" She seemed genuinely concerned as she dropped onto the couch.

"I meant to sleep here, but I was completely wasted and passed out."

"Why the couch? I wasn't even here." She dropped her eyes.

"Rose petals everywhere."

She flushed. "Oh. Yeah. I probably wouldn't have either."

Grayson sat down next to her. "Where did you sleep last night?"

She wouldn't meet his eyes. "I'll tell you, but you

have to let me finish explaining. It's not what it sounds like."

He wasn't sure he would like this, but he was willing to hear her out. He was willing to do just about anything to keep her in his life as his wife.

"I spent the night in Jeremy's room."

Anger bubbled up and he had to hold his temper in check. He was willing to do anything but share his wife with another man.

"Okay. I don't need to hear any more."

"Wait," she said and grabbed his arm. He hissed and jerked it away. Hurt crossed her face. Maybe he should've gone to the spa and taken care of the sunburn. "I need you to hear the rest of the story."

His tormented emotions roiled around inside of him. He didn't want to hear how she spent the night with Jeremy. But he owed her this much.

"Fine. But you have ten minutes, and then I'm going to the spa to see if they can help with the sunburn."

She nodded, staring at her hands. "I didn't sleep with Jeremy. We had the room attendant separate the beds. I slept in the room, but apart from him. I don't love him anymore, and I can't stand the thought of him touching me again. Not after what he did. He kissed me earlier, but I did not reciprocate, and I did not ask for it. I know it looked like it, but it wasn't.

Anyway, we did talk last night, and I understand now why you got so angry and don't really want to be married to me."

He definitely overacted when he saw her with Jeremy. He would have to think about how his emotions might affect her in the future. He didn't want her thinking things were over. "I may have gotten angry, but I definitely want to be married to you."

She met his eyes, tears in her own. "It's okay. You don't have to be a martyr. You slept with me, and that was enough for you to know that you didn't want to be with me. Jeremy was right about one thing. You are way above my league. I'll get over it."

Grayson had thought he'd taken care of this insecurity already, though he could see how she might come to that conclusion. He should've been thinking of her feelings instead of drowning in his own.

He scooted closer to her on the couch and took her hand into his.

"I got mad because I thought you hurt me. Because I couldn't stand the thought of you with another man and because I feared you'd chosen him over me. My own fear overrode my ability to understand your pain. I'm so very sorry. Dani, I want nothing more than to be your husband for the rest of my life."

He placed a soft kiss on her forehead. Then he

stood and headed upstairs. Dani didn't say anything. He found his bag and pulled out the marriage certificate and a pen and jogged back downstairs.

Dani wasn't there when he got there.

He looked around. She was out on the balcony. He gritted his teeth.

Fine. He could do this.

She glanced up when he came out.

"I thought you were going to the spa," she said, her voice still dejected.

He stared at her for just a minute. He couldn't believe he was so lucky as to have her. "I can do that later. I have a wife to take care of."

He took the chair across the table from her and set the certificate down. He signed first and then handed her the pen.

"Forever?" he asked. Nerves danced in his stomach. He wasn't sure if she'd say yes.

Tears flowed down her cheeks, and he wondered what he'd done wrong. "Are you okay?" he asked, leaning forward.

She nodded and gripped the pen. "You mean it?"

He pointed to his signature. "Yep. Your turn."

She didn't hesitate and signed her name.

They were officially husband and wife.

Forever.

EPILOGUE

*C*onner sipped his beer and glanced out at all of his friends playing on the beach, dogs and kids everywhere. Their group had grown significantly in the last few years. It seemed like everyone had found love and was settling down. It was the Fourth of July once again, and this time, Grayson and Dani decided to throw a housewarming party.

They bought a big house right on Lake Michigan with stunning views. Jessica sidled up next to him and slid her arm around his back.

"You know everyone is settling down," he said.

She squeezed his side. "We're settled down."

"We live in Dubai. That's hardly settled down."

"I like living in Dubai." She winked at him.

"Better than Cairo?" He did enjoy Dubai, but Cairo

was where they met, and it would always hold a special place in his heart.

She chuckled. "I don't know. I miss Cairo and its craziness. Plus, it will always hold a special place in my heart because that's where I met you. But I like our home in Dubai better."

"It's crazy to think that we've been together longer than all of them." And it was. Conner and Jessica were the first to get together.

Jessica grinned. "Yeah. I know. And they all have pretty cool love stories, but I think ours is the best."

"Me too."

Go back to where it all began in Pyramids and Promises...

Dear Reader,

Voyages and Vows originally had a completely different storyline, but one day I was coming home and listening to country music and a song popped up and suddenly it was different. And I love it so much.

If you've read all of the Michigan Millionaires books, you'll know that Jessica and Conner had the first love story. But I put their story at the end because the series began in my head with Tess and Lukas. But Conner's story is one that holds a special place in my heart. You can read it here: *Pyramids and Promises.*

As always if you loved the book or even if you didn't, please leave a review.

Thanks for being a fan,

Xoxo

Kim

P.S. Stay in touch!P.S. Stay in touch through my Kimberly Loth pen name!

1) I'm starting a text subscription service! If you sign up to get texts, you'll get:

• **6 FREE eBOOKS (all my 1st in series)!**

• **Exclusive alerts for all my sales, freebies & releases (you'll always be the first to know)!**

**To join, text BOOKS to (877) 949-4667.

See below for text disclaimers, including instructions for international fans.

2) We're going to spend the rest of the year having one big party to celebrate my upcoming releases. Come join us: **facebook.com/groups/Kimberly-LothReleaseParty**

Want More from Kimmy Loth?

Read about all the fraternity brothers in the Michigan Millionaires series

TEXT SERVICE DISCLAIMERS:

*excluding boxed sets
**You agree to receive automated promotional messages. This agreement isn't a condition of any purchase. Terms and Privacy Policy can be found at kimberlyloth.com/privacy. You may receive multiple messages month. Reply STOP to end or HELP for help.

This service is available for continental U.S. fans only, however international fans can join a NL group with the same promotions. For details email kimberly-lothteam@gmail.com

ALSO BY KIMMY LOTH

Michigan Millionaires (Sweet Romance Series)

Snowfall and Secrets

Folly and Forever

Monkeys and Mayhem

Michigan Millionaires Box Set Books 1-3

Roadtrips and Romance

Christmas and Commitment

Pyramids and Promises

Michigan Millionaires Box Set Books 4-6

Lakesides and Longing

ABOUT THE AUTHOR

Kimmy Loth has lived all over the world. From the isolated woods of the Ozarks to exotic city of Cairo. She currently lives on the beautiful Sugar Creek in southern Missouri with her sweet little dog, Maisy.

She's been writing for twelve years and also writes under the pen name Kimberly Loth. In her free time she volunteers at church, reads, and travels as often as possible.

She loves talking to school groups and book clubs. For more information about having her come speak at your school or event contact her at kimberlyloth@gmail.com.

Made in the USA
Monee, IL
11 August 2023

40686373R00121